My Second Life

"*My Second Life* is one of the finest debut YA novels I've ever read. The mystery at the heart of the book is utterly gripping, and I found myself reading more and more quickly, so desperate was I to find out the truth."

Anthony McGowan

My Second Life

Faye Bird

For
Reuben and Rosa

First published in the UK in 2014 by Usborne Publishing Ltd., Usborne House, 83-85 Saffron Hill, London EC1N 8RT, England. www.usborne.com

Cover photography: front cover photo © Serov/Shutterstock; back cover and spine © Anton Oparin/iStock/Thinkstock

A CIP catalogue record for this book is available from the British Library.

ISBN 9781409578604 03250/1 JFM MJJASOND/14

Printed in Chatham, Kent, UK.

prologue

The first time I was born, I was born Emma Trees. I was born to Amanda and Richard Trees. I was Emma. I was beautiful. People told me that. I had everything to live for. People told me that too. But I died. It was 18th October 1994. I was twenty-two.

And then I was born a second time, utterly against my will. Who knew you could be brought into the world twice, only six years after you left the first time? Who knew you could be born again and know – and I mean know like you know how to pull in the air and breathe – that you've been here and done all this before.

I was born Ana Ross on 28th June 2000. A millennium baby. And I thought I'd got away with missing all that millennium crap. I was born to Rachel Ross, and someone called David Summers, who has never shown up, which is okay because if I had two parents, two people who loved me as much as Rachel Ross loves me, I really don't think I could handle it. I feel kind of guilty that Rachel loves me so much, and thinks I'm so completely wonderful, when actually I've been here and done all this before with my first mum and dad. I do love Rachel. She just doesn't feel like Mum. Not to me. Amanda Trees is my mum, and she always will be.

The first time you're born it's pretty traumatic. A bit like being pulled out of a deliciously warm bath and being plonked wet and naked in the middle of the M25 in rush hour and someone saying, "GET ON WITH IT THEN!"

The second time I was born it was easier, because I knew the score. The rush of blind panic as you slip out, the first gasp of tight cold air, the hairy peering faces. I knew all that would pass, and that soon I'd be on the warm belly of someone I'd love for the rest of my life. Except when I looked up and saw Rachel, and she was looking down at me, smiling her tired puffy smile of love and exhaustion, all I could think was, *You're not my mum*, before someone wrapped me in a towel and placed a plump nipple into my mouth.

And that was it. I was off. I was living my second life. And there was nothing I could do about it, but live.

So I did.

I followed the pattern of each and every day, but this

time it was different, because this time I had a knowing sense of what was coming next. And I actually enjoyed childhood again a second time. It wasn't like I was bored or felt like I knew it all already. I mean, it's not like I knew everything – all the world's knowledge and all the world's secrets – from my first life anyway. One life lived is just that: one life lived. It's not every life.

I was quick to talk, and that was when things changed. Once I talked, once I could express myself, life began to feel somehow more fragmented. For a start, no one seemed to know my name.

"I'm Emma," I'd say as Rachel called "Ana" across the park when it was time to go home.

"I'm Emma!" I'd say when she called me "Ana Ross" and told me off for sticking my fingers in the peanut butter jar.

"Emma," I'd say as she sung me my bedtime song. I'd let her sing "Hush, Little Ana" all the way through, and I wouldn't ever interrupt. I'd wait until the end, and then I'd say it. I'd tell her my name was Emma, not Ana.

"Ana," she'd say back. "Darling, you're Ana. Ana. Night night," and she'd kiss me on the forehead and I'd want my mum, not Rachel, and I'd lie awake because it all felt so wrong. The wrongness of it was all I could feel.

* * *

I have never called Rachel "Mum". As soon as I learned to speak I called Rachel "Rachel".

She didn't like it.

"Please, Ana – call me 'Mum'!" she'd say.

But I couldn't.

Because it hurt too much to say the word "Mum" and see Rachel's face looking back at me, not my real mum's face; my first mum.

Eventually Rachel sort of accepted me calling her "Rachel", just as I had accepted her calling me "Ana", not Emma.

In this we were quits at least.

So here I am. Ana. Only one "n", which causes a huge amount of confusion throughout my life and generally draws attention in a way I really don't like that much. I'm fifteen years old, and I'm named after a Spanish Ana who Rachel went to school with, and whose name it seems just stuck in her memory. I don't know anything about Spanish Ana, but I do know that it kind of frustrates me that everyone is always spelling my name wrong, and I'm always having to correct them and spell it back, then explain about the Spanish Ana. It's like a curse, or one of my curses anyway.

And being Ana, well, it has good days and bad days, just like being anyone. To be honest, whole years have gone by when knowing that this is my second life hasn't even remotely bothered me. It is just how it has always been.

Until recently, that is.

Until I saw Frances.

And everything changed.

I'm not bipolar, in case you were wondering. I'm not manically depressed. I don't hallucinate, and there are no voices in my head. There is no Emma voice telling me to do stuff. I think I would know if I was ill, or someone would have told me, or suggested I see a doctor or a therapist or something. I've never been arrested for strange behaviour in the street. I've never even had a detention. I think I'm pretty normal for a fifteen-year-old girl: I go to school; I do my homework; I've got mates – Zak, Hannah and Jamie, a few others. I'm not one of those people who likes to hang out in a clique or a crowd. I had a best mate in Ellie, but she moved to the States. And of course I've got Rachel, and my grandma, Grillie. I fight with Rachel, but that's normal…right? To fight with your parent? And my vice? If you can call it that. Well, I've got a thing about Converse. I have three pairs – blue, purple and green – and I'm aiming to own a pair in every colour.

And that's it.

That's me – Ana.

I'm Ana.

And it's just that I was Emma, before. So I know more about the world than I should for a person my age. I guess you could say that's a shame, but what I know is so random, mixed up, that until I saw Frances it really didn't matter what I knew. It was just the varied stuff of a life that had been lived before. So I know what it feels like to taste Kalamata olives and unripe avocados before I put them into my mouth…and I know what it feels like to down pints of cider and black… The thrill of hailing a cab in New York… The utter joy of a first kiss with someone you've been waiting to touch and to hold and be held by. I could probably roll a joint if you passed me the Rizlas. But it doesn't ruin life knowing these things. It hasn't ruined it at all.

And how do I know them? I'm not sure that's something I'll ever truly understand. Even when life has been full of recognition, there's still always been room for discovery. And I thought that was a good thing. But when I saw Frances in the hospital, my whole life fell apart. It disintegrated like lit tissue paper in my hands. Because in seeing Frances I remembered what I did in my first life.

And what I did was kill a person. And to discover that – to discover the ugly memories of that – to remember some of what you did – but not all that happened – it is hell. And it is what happened to me.

monday

1.

"We're going to see Grillie later. You have remembered, haven't you?" Rachel shouted through the bathroom door to me as I stepped out of the shower.

"Yes! What time is her op?"

"They said it'll be sometime this morning. I can call at midday and we can go from three onwards. I'll pick you up from school."

"That's fine!" I shouted back.

Except I remembered that I'd said I'd meet Jamie after school. We'd arranged to go for a coffee. Jamie was my friend, but I'd *liked* him for ages. For months. He'd been going out with this girl in my year, Melissa, over the summer, but when we got back to school last week there were rumours going round that they'd broken up. I was there when Zak asked Jamie what had happened – he had just said Melissa was "no fun". I could have told him that and then he wouldn't have had to go out with her. But I didn't say anything. I just laughed, and then quickly suggested we go to the cafe after school the next day. And now I'd have to text him and let him know I couldn't make it. I wanted to see Grillie after her operation, but...it was gutting. Really gutting.

I sighed, wrapped my towel around me and opened the bathroom door and found myself face-to-face with Rachel more suddenly than I'd anticipated.

"Didn't realize you were still standing right *there*!" I said impatiently as I nipped past her and made my way into my room.

She tutted and started to head downstairs.

"I'll meet you at the gates, okay?" she shouted back.

"Okay!"

I looked at my phone to see if I had any messages.

Nothing.

I texted Jamie.

Can't make the cafe today. Got to see my gran.
Tomorrow? Ax

Grillie – my grandma Millie – was old. Eighty-two years old. When I was younger I would sit on her lap for hours on long weekend afternoons and I would stroke her soft cheek, and sing with her, and wonder whether she'd ever lived before. It was only because she was old. And wise. The oldest and wisest person I knew.

They say that wisdom comes with age, don't they? I worked out in the shower this morning that between my two lives, my cumulative age was thirty-seven. Weird. Thirty-seven years of living, and really I was none the wiser.

When Rachel picked me up after school she was really anxious. When we got to the hospital she pounded the corridors as we followed the signs towards the ward.

"Are you okay, Rachel?"

"Yes, yes. I just want to see her, that's all."

"It was just a routine operation, wasn't it?"

"Yes, but she's eighty-two. There are always risks when you're eighty-two."

"What did they say when you phoned earlier?"

"They said it went well."

"That's good, isn't it?"

"Yes."

"But you're thinking that's what they always say. But you never really know until you get here."

Rachel slowed her pace and looked at me. "Exactly," she said, and she stroked my hair as we walked and I wanted to pull away from her as she touched me. It just made me want Mum even more when she touched me. Her loss was like an endless ache when I was with Rachel. It was something I'd always lived with. It was with me almost all the time. But today I let Rachel stroke my hair. I didn't pull away. Because I didn't want to hurt her feelings. Not now when she was so worried about Grillie.

When we walked into the ward Grillie was sat up in bed. She smiled when she saw us. I could see it was a struggle to smile. Even though she was propped up she didn't look all that comfortable. She had a crinkly gown on and a blanket wrapped around her shoulders. She was pale but calm. I knew she wasn't going to die. Not today.

"How are you?" Rachel said, leaning forwards to give her a kiss.

I wanted to give her a kiss too, to say hello, but I was nervous. I didn't want to lean in and press down on her in all the wrong places.

"My throat's a little dry," she said.

I jumped to it. "Here, I'll pour you some water." There was a plastic jug on the side with a flappy white lid and a small plastic cup.

"Thank you, lovely," she said.

I sat down gently on the side of the bed, passing her the cup. She took a drink and then she set the cup down and took my hand.

"So how was your day, lovely?" she said.

"Oh – not much to tell. Just school," I said.

"But you like it, don't you? It's a good school. Rachel's always telling me how well you're doing."

I looked at Grillie. She was tired. Her usual feisty chat dulled by the painkillers. She was slow, placid.

"I'm going to go and find a nurse. See if we can get you another pillow," said Rachel. "I'll be back in a minute."

"How long do you have to stay in for?" I asked.

"Not sure just yet. See how I go. If all is well I'll be out by the weekend, I think."

"I'll come again tomorrow, yeah? Bring you a magazine or something."

"Yes. I'd like that," she said and then her hand slipped its grip from mine and she sank quickly into sleep. I knew it was the drugs but it still surprised me.

Rachel came back.

"She's asleep," I whispered.

"Oh – is she?" Rachel said. I could see the disappointment in her face as she pulled the pillow she'd just found for Grillie towards her tummy. She was hugging it to her, for comfort.

"I'm sure she'll wake up again in a minute," I said. I wanted to make it better for her.

"I don't know. She must be tired. And all the drugs… she needs to sleep."

I stood up to let Rachel sit where I had been sitting on the bed, and I went and pulled around the curtain to give Grillie some privacy. I watched Rachel put the pillow down and take Grillie's hand, and as she held it in her own she looked into Grillie's face with such love. I had never felt love like that for Rachel. Because all I have ever wanted is my mum. My real mum. I wanted to cry and call out for her now, to come to me. But I couldn't. Because no one would have come.

The room suddenly felt hot.

Too hot.

"Maybe you're right. Maybe we should go?" I said to Rachel, picking up my bag from the floor. "We should let her sleep."

I had to get out. Find some fresh air. I had to get out, to breathe.

"Yes," said Rachel, and she picked up the pillow she'd left on the end of the bed and plumped it before putting it back, and then she kissed Grillie on the forehead, so gently, and we left.

We walked through the hospital in complete silence. I didn't know why I felt so bad. Maybe it was just the hospital. There was a smell of illness in the air. A place where you went to get better should smell of good health – of a rich, dark earth and a fresh spring wind – but this place smelled sterile and poisonous. I kept walking, fast, trying to get Rachel to walk faster with me. I could tell she was worried, thinking hard. Her pace was much slower than when we'd arrived. And as I walked I looked at the walls, the signs, the people here visiting family, friends…

I could see a rush up ahead: a couple of doctors with a trolley jogging it along the corridor, people parting ways. An emergency. *Just let me out. Let me out…* That's all I could think as I kept walking. The trolley was coming closer now, and I could see there was an old woman lying on it, crying, her arms stretched high on a pillow above her head, her head turned to one side. Crying. Wailing. I stopped. I had to. I was forced to. And as much as I didn't want to look, I did. And that's when I saw her – Frances. She opened her eyes as she passed me, and we were locked together in a moment—

"Frances Wells…" I said, out loud, as they wheeled her away.

"What's that?" said Rachel.

"That was Frances Wells!"

I knew her… I knew her face.

An image flew through my mind: a child, a small child, with her eyes open wide…wet and wild…her body, still… cradled by a mass of twigs and branches in the water.

I thought I might pass out. I took a deep breath in.

"She didn't look so well, did she?" said Rachel, utterly mishearing me.

"Let's go, come on," said Rachel. "Let's get fish and chips."

And as we walked out into the cooler air I could feel that something had changed. There had been a shift –

in me – and I had this feeling. A feeling that I had done something so wrong… So very wrong that I didn't dare to name it… And I was afraid.

tuesday

2.

I went back to visit Grillie the following day. She was better: less pale, her eyelids less droopy. She was offering me strawberries and interrupting me all the time, so I knew she was on her way to being well again. The curtain was drawn around us as we sat and talked, and she was impatient to tell me all the details of the ward, about who was who and who'd said what.

"The one next door," she mouthed in a theatrical whisper, pointing in the direction of the next bed. I nodded to stop her pointing and mouthing the words. "She's in a terrible state. Terrible. Been up all night crying with the pain."

I could tell Grillie was kind of enjoying the drama of it all. "Did you sleep all right, though?"

"Me? Oh yes. Fine. I woke up a couple of times, you know, with the noise" – and again she pointed – "but generally I slept fine. Can't wait to get home now. Get back into my own bed. And the food is pretty awful."

"Rachel's made you a pie, for when you get home. Chicken. It's in the freezer."

"Oh, lovely," she said. "I'll look forward to that."

We sat in silence for a moment. I could hear a voice, a doctor, talking to the woman in the opposite bed. Something about tests and needing to go down to the ground floor, and a porter coming in about an hour.

"Open the curtain a little, lovely. Just in case the doctor's got anything to say to me too."

I stood up to open the curtain and smiled to myself. I knew Grillie just wanted a good nosey at everyone else. I didn't blame her. There wasn't much else to do, and I'd forgotten to buy the magazine I'd promised.

"Shall I go down and get you that magazine?" I said.

"Don't bother, honestly. I can't really concentrate on anything for too long at the moment. Reading just sends me to sleep. I'm fine. Just open the curtain some more. Get the light in here. I'd have liked a bed right next to the window. Lots of light. But they put me here. A bed by the window would have been nice, wouldn't it?"

"A room with a view," I said, smiling. "Yes, that would have been nice, Grillie. Very nice." And as I walked the curtain all the way around the bed and pushed it firmly against the wall I saw the person in the bed next to Grillie's – next to where I stood. Frances Wells. She was still, motionless. I was close enough to reach out and touch her.

My body tensed up until all I could feel was the pain as my muscles contracted hard under my skin. If I could have pulled myself inwards and retracted, into nothing, I would have done it. A sickness was rising up from my belly, slowly, steadily.

She'd been the one wailing all night. She'd been the one in pain. It was Frances Wells. And she didn't know that I was here – now – that I had been Emma.

My chest pounded as the sickness travelled upwards towards my throat. I tried to swallow it down, and as I did I was filled with a stark and vivid memory. I was outside a house. A big house. Frances was inside. I could see her through the window. She was younger, smiling, happy… She wore a navy dress with red stitching and red buttons and a shiny thick black belt. Her hair was tied back but strands were hanging down in front of her ears, and around her collar. She was pretty. She was stood in a large front room. There were dark green sofas, and bookshelves, a fireplace… There was someone else in the room with her. A man. He was standing behind her and she was talking to him, telling him something. They were laughing. And she stepped forwards and she closed the curtains. Her neat, slim waist was the last thing I saw through the final gap of the closing material in the window as she turned away from me and disappeared into the depths of the room. I didn't want her to close the curtains. I could feel anger pulsing in my chest… She'd shut me out. Why had she shut me out?

"Ana?" Grillie's voice broke through.

I hung on to Grillie's bed. I grasped the cold metal bar on the headboard until it hurt all the way up my arms. I couldn't let myself be sick. Not here. Not now. I tried to swallow again and my mouth was wet, too wet. I could feel the rising lumps in my throat, the banging in my ears. I screwed up my eyes, and I opened my mouth wide to gulp some air and as I did my shoulders sunk down and I felt the banging in my body begin to slowly subside. I let go of the bed and looked down at Frances again. I couldn't help myself looking.

She was an old woman. She lay on her side sleeping. Her body now wider, heavier with age, her hair shorter, colourless, wiry, although it still settled on her neck like it used to. It was her. It was Frances. I knew her. It was actually her.

"Ana? Are you okay?" Grillie was shifting in her bed behind me. I could hear the sheets slipping around her as she moved.

I looked at Grillie and I tried a smile.

"She doesn't look well, does she?" Grillie said, motioning towards Frances with her head.

"Have you talked to her?"

"Yes," Grillie said. "She's in a lot of pain."

"Has she had any visitors?" I whispered.

Grillie shook her head. "No one."

I looked over my shoulder again. I wanted to make sure Frances was still asleep, that she couldn't hear a word of what we were saying.

"Lost a husband to cancer, and then a daughter. The child drowned. She was only six years old."

I nodded. I didn't feel like I could speak. I swallowed and my throat felt thick again, like it was swelling, but this time with tears. I didn't know where to look so I walked away and took a chair from under the window. It gave me some time to breathe, and then I brought it over to sit next to Grillie on the other side of the bed.

Guilt.

All I could feel was guilt.

It was uncoiling itself inside of me.

"She told you that?" I whispered.

"I only asked whether she had any children. I wondered if she was going to have any visitors. That other woman over there, she's got people coming in left, right and centre. It's like a bloody bus station…"

I nodded again.

"…She told me she had a daughter, and I jumped in and said how nice that was and that I had a daughter and a granddaughter, that you were both coming in later and what a blessing it was… And then she said she'd lost her child, her daughter. I felt terrible. I mean, how was I to know? Terrible. And then she told me very matter-of-factly that the girl had been drowned, when she was only six years old…"

I took Grillie's hand. "You couldn't have known, Grillie."

"I know that, but I felt awful…and then the worst of it was I couldn't think of anything else to say. Shut me right up, it did. Until I started gabbling to fill in the awkward silence. I ended up inviting her to bridge. I wish I hadn't. So I'm glad to see you, Ana, because I haven't been able to talk to anyone else today, but her. I'm not talking to Mrs Popular over there, so maybe you should go and get me that magazine, lovely? Something gossipy and fun."

"Did she say anything else? About her daughter?" I asked.

Grillie was fumbling with her purse, trying to find some coins. "No, nothing else, lovely. And I didn't like to ask. Now here, get yourself something too. Some chocolate or something…"

I took the coins and walked down to the shop. I glanced back at Frances's motionless body as I went. This was the closest I had ever been to my first life, and I didn't know what I was meant to do. But in that very moment I was glad of the space to think, of the opportunity to be walking away.

3.

I was meeting Jamie at four thirty.

I couldn't stop thinking about Frances Wells as I walked to meet him at the cafe.

I walked, and I thought.

I was a good person, wasn't I?

There had been times when I was desperate to tell someone how I'd lived before, but I never did. I'd held on to my secret to protect the people I loved. That was good, wasn't it? That had been the right thing to do? I was trying to be a good person. But now – Frances – and these memories – this feeling of shame – and guilt – I didn't know what to do with that—

42 The Avenue.

It came to me, as I walked, like someone had posted a letter to my brain.

42 The Avenue.

It was there, suddenly.

42 The Avenue.

An address.

Frances's address.

I was sure.

Jamie was late.

It shouldn't have mattered. Going out with Jamie for a coffee after school was actually pretty normal. But now that my best mate Ellie had moved away and Zak was going out with Hannah, our gang had dwindled to almost nothing. Now there was just me and Jamie and it felt, well, awkward. I liked him too much. Way too much. And I wasn't sure I could hide it if the others weren't there.

I ordered a hot chocolate with whipped cream, marshmallows – the lot – and sat down on the sofas next to a low table by the window. I played with the spoon, looking up every now and then to see if he'd arrived. I picked up my phone. No messages. I flicked through my photos, my contacts, and then I opened up a Web search and put in 42 The Avenue Frances Wells. I didn't remember where I'd lived before. Frances being here, now, didn't give me anything to go on. Not really. I could have lived anywhere before. But I put in London anyway. It seemed like a good place to start. I scanned the pages. Nothing. A few people called Frances who'd lived on Avenues. Of course. What was I thinking? Like it was going to give me some kind of information on…what? What was I looking for exactly? I didn't know… Some proof, I guess – that Frances was who I thought she was.

"Sorry, I know I'm late."

Jamie was here.

"Hi!" I said, overenthusiastically, putting away my phone.

"I'm gonna get one of those too!" he said, pinching a marshmallow off the top of my mug, and then he walked up to the queue to order.

I looked over at him and popped a pink marshmallow into my mouth and sucked it soft while I waited for him to come back and sit down. He looked nice.

"So, you all right?"

I felt awkward.

"Yeah, yes," I said.

"How's your gran?"

"Yeah," I said. "Yeah, she's okay. She'll be home soon."

"That's good," he said, spooning whipped cream into his mouth. "Mmm, this too." He looked up and smiled at me, his eyes sort of holding mine. I wasn't sure whether to look away or carry on looking back at him, but somehow I couldn't let go of his gaze.

"What did you do last night then?" I asked, racking my brains for something – anything – to say.

"Went to Zak's, played Xbox…"

"That's all you two ever do!"

"No, it's not!" he said. "Anyway, I didn't hang around for long – Hannah turned up."

If Zak wasn't playing Jamie on the Xbox then he was basically pretty much guaranteed to be getting loved up with Hannah.

"You should come to Zak's next time," Jamie said. "You'd make me feel like less of a third wheel."

"Yeah, right!" I said. "Thanks!"

I looked at my phone – I wasn't sure why – then at Jamie again.

When he looked back at me I felt a rise and fall. It was as if he'd lifted me up and then gently set me down again. But I hadn't moved at all. He'd done that with his eyes. I felt hot inside.

"Have you heard from Ellie?" I said, trying to change the subject, break the moment.

"Nah," he said. "It's been what, a couple of weeks?"

"Four," I said. "Nearly five."

"She's probably busy. You know, settling into her glamorous new life in the US of A." He grinned at me as he said it.

I smiled.

"I'm sure you'll hear from her soon," he said.

His eyes were blue; more blue than I remembered.

Beautifully blue.

"So are you going out tonight?" he asked.

I shook my head and picked up my mug, staring into the bottom of it. It was virtually empty now; I took a sip of foamy air.

"What's up, Ana?"

"Nothing..."

"You don't seem yourself."

I wasn't being myself. I knew that. He knew that.

"I'm fine, really."

"So come out then," he said. "Come out with me and Zak. We're going over to Sammy's tonight."

"Maybe. I don't know. I'll have to check with Rachel. It's a school night—"

"Tell her you're coming to mine, to study."

"Yeah – maybe—"

As I broke off I could see he was hanging on for my answer, searching my eyes for a "yes", and I wondered for a split second whether I could tell him. Could I tell him that in the hospital bed next to my Grillie there was this seriously old woman I'd known before from my first life, the life I'd lived before this one, the life only I knew about, the life that I'd kept a secret from him, from Ellie, from them all. I was desperate, suddenly, to say it out loud, to tell him, there and then, and just shout it, scream it—

And there it was again. The little girl's face in the water. She was in a river. Pale, still, her eyes open and wide – the river so dark it was black – her clothes so bright in the water. She was floating.

"Just tell her we need to work on a presentation or something," Jamie said.

And I looked back at him.

"I can't, Jamie. I wish I could but I can't." And as I said it, I thought I saw a flicker of disappointment in his eyes, reflecting the disappointment that I knew was crouching quietly in mine. But all I could think about in that moment was Frances Wells and the shape of her body between the curtains in the dusk, and my anger, my fury, that she'd shut me out – that she'd left me outside the house – that she'd left me outside to play – and that there was no one I could tell. There was no one.

wednesday

4.

Double chemistry. Double maths. Wednesday was officially the worst day of the week.

I pretty much doodled all the way through chemistry. Well, perhaps not all the way through. I took down the notes, copied out what I needed to, but I didn't actually think about any of it, or answer any of the questions. Instead, I doodled. And I did the same in maths too. I was trying to block out the image of the dead girl, lying face up in the water, her skirt puffed out around her sides. It didn't matter where I put the pencil on the paper I just kept drawing lines that turned into trees and branches that turned into reflections on the river that turned into her hair as it floated outwards from her little head. I'd turn the page and start again and all I could see was her wet hair spread out against the bank, her face pale, open and shocked. She was dead, but somehow still alive enough to look like she might, at any moment, simply sit up and blink, and ask me why...why had I killed her?

Because I had.

I'd killed her.

I'd killed that little girl.

I felt a pain so clear and sharp in my stomach that I thought I was going to be sick.

"I feel sick. Can I go?"

I stood up.

"Do you think you are actually going to be sick, Ana?" asked Mr Roberts.

I nodded and started walking towards the classroom door so Mr Roberts had no choice but to let me go.

I'd killed her.

I didn't remember how or when, but I could see her face, as I'd seen it then, and I knew she was in that river because of me. I might not have remembered leaving her to cough and splutter as her lungs filled up, until there was not a breath of her left, but I knew right down to my core that I'd killed her, that I was guilty. And I couldn't get the image of her face in the water out of my mind.

I didn't go to the toilets.

I walked straight out of school and into the street and I just kept walking. I wasn't really sure where I was going. I felt less sick now that I was outside. I guessed the school would call Rachel once they'd realized that I had gone. I'd never bunked before. I didn't really know how these things worked. I had been in for registration. Maybe no one would notice that I had gone. I looked at my watch. It was just after midday…

It was just after midday and I had killed a person.

I had to keep going, keep walking towards the Tube, get away. It was all I could think to do. The pain was there again. I held on to my side and I felt my heart speed up.

I had killed a person.

A child.

I got to Richmond station, jumped onto the Tube and sat down.

There was a buzz in my pocket.

A text.

Rachel.

Just got a call from the hospital. Grillie's coming out. Going home now to pick up some things for her and then to hospital to take her home. I'll be late. Pizza in the fridge. x

I put my phone away. She didn't know I'd bunked. Not yet.

I changed at Gloucester Road.

I got on the Circle line.

All trains lead to Edgware Road All trains lead to Edgware Road All trains lead to Edgware Road… I could feel my eyes getting heavier… It was soothing here…

safe...I could feel normal here...I was just sitting on the Tube like everybody else...and wherever I went I would never be lost...I would never be lost...I would never...

The little girl was wearing black patent shoes and white tights. The tights were new; they were clean and bright and stiff at the seams. They were poking out through the gaps in her shoes. I helped her with the shoes. She said she didn't like the way they felt. So I took them off and I straightened the tights. I tucked the seams under her toes, and slipped them back on her feet. She looked so pleased to be dressed up, but still so uncomfortable. A red skirt and a cream blouse, with a cream ribbon at the neck. Nothing like anyone would wear these days. Her clothes were prim, and straight and a bit static. Her hair was parted in the middle and clipped up high above her ears with tartan bows on each side. I could see her, looking at me, smiling.

"You look silly, dressed like that, Catherine."

That's what I said to her.

Catherine.

I was in my favourite outfit. Dungarees and a long-sleeved Snoopy T-shirt. We were across the road from the house on The Avenue, standing on the Green opposite number 42. A red-brick house with a clean white tile hung on the porch wall, decorated with glazed red numbers. 42. There was a pretty pattern around the edges of the numbers too. It was raised, bumpy. I remembered running my fingers along its swirls and curls—

"You okay there?"

I'd fallen asleep.

"Where are you going?"

It was a woman with bright red lipstick and a severe fringe. Her face was way too close to mine. For a minute I couldn't see where I was. She was touching my shoulder, trying to wake me.

"Yeah, I'm fine. Thanks," I said.

And I saw I was at Edgware Road. I had to change. I stepped off the Tube and crossed over to the next Circle line train waiting on the opposite platform. I'd go around. I'd go right around and back to Gloucester Road again.

I closed my eyes.

The Green was a piece of common land, with some trees. I could see it so clearly in my mind. The houses on The Avenue overlooked the Green, and beyond it, the Thames. The Avenue was a quiet place. A quiet road with twenty or so houses, the common land, and direct access across the Green down to the river. It was peaceful.

"We're going to the river, Catherine. We'll play hide-and-seek at the river."

I'd said that.

And all the time I was waiting for my dad. I wanted my dad to come and play, like he'd said he would. But he never came. And I could still feel the anger that I felt because he never came.

My heart started beating faster.

I felt hot.

I coughed and opened my eyes to check where I was.

We were moving slowly through a tunnel. I closed my eyes again.

I willed for something more to come. Nothing.

I could feel a pain – in my head – a pressure, building.

Where was my dad?

I looked up again to see where I was.

I couldn't settle.

The pain was hovering over my eyes now, crawling over my scalp.

Embankment.

I'd killed her.

The little girl. Catherine. I'd killed her.

I held my hands up to cradle my head...to soothe the pain.

I could just about see the sign. Embankment. It was definitely Embankment.

I was a good person, wasn't I? I'd always been a good person.

Did I have to pay for what I'd done?

I screwed my eyes shut.

Is that why I was here again? To pay?

I squeezed my eyes shut – tighter still – there was only pain.

I had to get rid of the pain. I had to.

My head felt like it was going to explode. A constant high-pitched tone in my ears was drowning out the rattle of the Tube. Every movement of the carriage hurt me… every rock and turn… I'd seen Frances – and now this. Was it only ever a matter of time? Frances and the memories, the feelings, this knowledge – that I'd killed Catherine – it must have all been sitting there, like a tumour growing quietly on the brain. And now – now I had to find a way to stop it, to nuke it, shrink it, make it go away… I wanted to scream out with the pain, with the fear, with the feeling that I might just explode into a thousand tiny pieces if I did nothing. If I just sat there and did nothing…

Gloucester Road.

A voice told me it was Gloucester Road.

I had to change

I had to go now.

To the hospital.

I had to see Frances.

It was the only thing I could do.

And as soon as I had the thought – as soon as I decided that I would go and see her – the pain lifted slightly, and I was certain that it was the right thing to do.

5.

The closer I got to the hospital the more sick I felt. The pressure had lessened in my head, but the black feelings, they were all still there. When I walked up to the nurses' station in the ward my hands were visibly shaking. I didn't want to see any of the same nurses I'd seen when I was here visiting Grillie.

"Who are you here to see then, my love?" the nurse said. She was new. She didn't know who I was and as I went to answer my mouth was dry as a pit. The words felt like they were stuck to my lips.

"Frances Wells… I'm her niece," I lied.

The nurse said how nice it would be for Frances to have a visitor, how Frances hadn't had any visitors since she'd been in, and the nurse kept on talking as we made our way through the ward. I was only half listening because I could see Frances now. She was sat strong and upright in bed, reading. She looked better, better than she had before. She glanced up at me, and then back at her book, smoothing a cloth bookmark between her fingers as she read.

She didn't look up again.

She clearly hadn't seen me, or recognized me, but then she had always been asleep when I'd visited before.

I wished she would recognize me. If she recognized me – if she saw something in me that reminded her of Emma – then she would be more likely to believe me. I was sure of that. I wasn't as beautiful as Emma. I knew that. People told me I was beautiful when I was Emma. They didn't do that now. But maybe, just maybe, something – my eyes, my voice – would remind her of Emma.

"I'm not sure that she'll recognize me," I said to the nurse as we neared the bed. "It's been quite a long time."

"I'll leave you to it then, my love," she said, and she left.

"Hello," I said.

Frances looked up at me. She didn't speak.

"I'm Millie's granddaughter. Millie who was here, in the bed next to you," and I pointed.

"Yes," she said. "I know Millie." She was very clear, very definite with her words. I couldn't tell what she was thinking.

I felt so nervous. I'd never felt this nervous about anything before.

There was a pause.

"You know Millie's gone home now, don't you?" she said.

"Yes, yes I do. I...I came to see you."

I was stumbling over my words now. I swallowed, to try and calm myself down, to get some saliva in my mouth.

"To see me?" Frances said.

"Yes."

"Why?"

My legs started to shake uncontrollably.

"Can I sit down?"

Frances nodded to the chair next to her bed. There was a white plastic bag full of wool and needles on the chair. "Move that bag – here..." She motioned for me to pass it over to her, then set it down on the bed and put her book on the bedside table. Everything she did was very slow, ordered. She didn't take her eyes off me once and her fingers, resting on the edge of the sheet, were constantly rubbing the material between her forefinger and her thumb, as if for comfort.

"Do I know you?" she said.

And my heart beat so loudly when she said it that my chest shuddered in response.

"Yes. I think so," I said. "That's why I came back – to see you. Because – because I think I know you. I mean...when I saw you here, in the bed next to Grillie...I knew who you were."

"Right," she said. And I felt cold now. So cold I was shivering. But I had to keep talking. I had to.

"You lived in The Avenue, didn't you?" I said.

"Yes," she said. "I still do."

My heart bashed my chest again. I could feel the blood rushing around my body, or was it adrenalin? Whatever it was, I didn't like it. I pressed my hands together in my lap to stop them lifting up towards my heart. I wanted to protect my heart, cup it, soften the bashing, make it slow. If Frances still lived there now in the house I remembered, and she was in hospital here, then The Avenue couldn't be that far away.

If I was this close to Frances, to where she had lived, where she still lived now, could I be close to my mum too? Could I be close enough to find her? To see her? And Dad?

"You've lived there a long time," I said, trying to hide the weakness in my voice.

"Forty-five years next April," she said and she looked at me with a stare that was utterly unreadable. And I realized that the whole time we'd been speaking she hadn't blinked. Not once. "Do you live nearby? I've never seen you. I'm quite sure."

I shook my head.

And I said it –

"I knew your daughter."

I just said it.

And I held my breath, after I did, to hold on to the sob that was rising in my chest.

"Millie told me that she lives on Connaught Gardens. That's close by. Perhaps we've seen each other, in the street."

"No – I knew your daughter!" I cried out, standing up as I spoke.

Frances paused before she answered, her eyes still firmly fixed on mine.

"I heard you the first time," she said. "Now sit down."

I sat automatically, at her command.

"I...I know it sounds like the most unlikely, most unbelievable thing you've ever heard," I said, "but—"

"My daughter died thirty-three years ago. Thirty – three – years." She repeated the words, pronouncing every syllable, as if the pain of all those years was encapsulated in each and every sound.

"I know, but..." I had to tell her I was Emma. I had to tell her. If I couldn't tell *her*, then there was no one I could tell. No one.

"I'd like you to leave now," she said.

"Don't make me leave!" I said. "I've got to talk to you." Suddenly, I was desperate.

A nurse approached the bed with a fresh water jug and said how nice it was that Frances had a visitor and how she must be pleased. Frances just nodded and smiled. I waited for the nurse to leave. It felt like an age, but eventually she went. And then Frances spoke again.

"Memory is a strange thing," she said. "I'd say you've seen me before, round and about, but you just haven't remembered, until now."

"No! That's not it – it's not—" My voice was getting louder now.

"Your grandma lives near me. You've probably seen me somewhere in Teddington when you were visiting her."

"No!" I said again. "It's not that—"

"My memory plays tricks on me all the time," Frances said, interrupting me, slow and strong. And as she spoke she cast her eyes around the ward as if she were looking for someone to call over, to raise an alarm. Was she going to call security? Was she going to get me removed? I panicked.

"Please – please," I said. "I want to talk to you about Catherine—" and my voice cracked as I said her name. "Please—" I was leaning forwards now, speaking in an urgent half-whisper. "Please—"

Frances turned her head back towards me and looked straight into my eyes. It was a hard look.

"I was Catherine's mother," she said. "Once. A very long time ago. But as I told you, she died."

"I know," I said. It was all I could think to say.

"Did Millie tell you?" she asked.

"What?"

"About Catherine."

"She told me you'd lost your daughter."

"And that's why you're here?"

"Well, yes…no… I knew already… That's why I'm here. Because I knew."

"I don't know how you could have known Catherine. I don't even know how you know her name. I never told Millie her name." And she looked suddenly pale, pale as paper, and I was scared. I didn't want to hurt her. I didn't want to make her ill again.

I shouldn't have come. What was I thinking? I panicked.

"I shouldn't have come," I said. "I'm sorry. I'm so sorry." And I stood up and reached out and touched her hand, to try and make better what I'd said, what I'd done by coming here, and as I did I was shocked by a sudden tightening in my chest. I felt like I was being squeezed from the outside in, tighter and tighter, and I opened my mouth to try and pull in some air, but the air, it was less and less clear to breathe. I couldn't grasp a breath, not even one, and I thought my chest would cave in with the trying. I pulled my hand away from Frances's – and a breath came to me. I felt the oxygen seeping back into my lungs, my chest, rising and falling in relief. The panic subsided.

"I have to go," I said.

Frances didn't speak. She just watched me. She watched

me as I walked out of the ward, out of her sight, and as soon as I was, I broke into a run. I ran through the corridors, down the cold stairwell and I didn't stop until I was outside in the bright and natural light of day.

I sat on the wall in front of the main entrance of the hospital and put my head between my knees.

I was immediately and urgently sick, all over the pavement between my feet.

I raised my head to pull my hair out of my eyes and to wipe my mouth. People walked by, but no one came over, and I was glad. I didn't want to see or speak to anyone. I just wanted to be alone, to be away from everyone. To cry and cry and cry.

But the tears, they wouldn't come.

6.

I walked home. It took me an hour. I was tired and my body felt heavy. Three buses passed me, but I didn't care. However tired and emotionally sick I felt now, I had to be alone. I couldn't sit with a stranger on the bus, and I couldn't go home. I'd suffocate in my own sadness if I did. I'd been so close to my first life. I'd reached out and touched it. I'd never dared to think that it would have been possible before. But now it was, and it wasn't in any way what I'd wanted it to be.

I felt my phone vibrate in my bag as I turned into our road. It was a text. Jamie.

I didn't see you this afternoon. You OK?

I put my phone back in my bag and opened the front door and went straight up to my room. I needed to avoid Rachel. I quietly closed my bedroom door and slid down to sit with my back against it. Rachel called out a "Hello".

"Hi!" I shouted back, trying to hide the upset in my voice.

"You want something to eat? I've done us lasagne."

"I'll be down in a minute."

I pulled my phone out of my bag and looked at Jamie's text again. He wanted to know if I was okay. He didn't normally send me texts asking whether I was okay.

I closed my eyes.

I wanted to cry but still, nothing would come.

I screwed my eyes shut and held my breath, like I could wring out a tear, force something out of me, but all I could think about, in that moment, was Jamie and the way he'd looked at me yesterday in the cafe.

Thinking about Jamie felt good.

Better than anything else.

I opened my eyes, looked at my phone and texted him back.

Went home sick. OK now. See you tomorrow.

"It's on the table!" Rachel's voice came up the stairs.

"I'm coming!" I got up off the floor and looked at myself in the mirror. I grabbed my brush and pulled it through my hair so that I didn't look so weird. I rubbed my face with my hands, as if I could wipe away the sadness and confusion. But it was all over me. So I tried a smile – a fake one, a practice – and I headed down.

"Are you all right?" Rachel asked as soon as she saw me.

"Yeah," I said, sitting down at the table.

"You're flushed." She stood up and put her hand on my forehead, like she did when I was small. I looked up at her and saw Mum. Not Rachel, but Mum. My first mum. Her soft blonde hair and her twinkly eyes, and I felt sick with the loss of her.

"You haven't got a temperature," Rachel said. "Do you feel okay?"

"I'm not that hungry actually," I said, pushing my plate away from me. The smell of the food made me want to gag. "Do you mind if I just go up to bed?"

"Sure. Do you want anything?"

"I'm just tired, I think."

"Well, go up then. I'll come up in a bit and see how you are."

I climbed into bed with all my clothes on and I wrapped the duvet around me. It felt comforting and I was warm. I closed my eyes and turned myself over onto my back, ready to try and feign sleep. It felt like a familiar thing to do, to lie down, to close my eyes, to shut out the world. I knew I'd lain like this many times before when I was Emma, I'd buried myself in duvets and blankets – cocoon-like – and it was reassuring. I could hear Rachel scraping the plates, and the general kitchen clatter below me as she loaded the dishwasher and I knew she'd be up soon.

And then the phone rang downstairs. Rachel answered. It was Grillie. I could tell it was her from the way Rachel chatted on about her day. And then she was quieter, listening. “Right,” she said. “Okay… Who…? What do you mean…? Today?” There was a pause. “Right… I’ll talk to her and let you know… Of course…”

And then she hung up, and I lay still and closed my eyes, waiting for her. But she never came to check on me like she said she would.

thursday

7.

When I got up the next day I was completely starving. I'd slept in my uniform. I should have put on a clean shirt, clean tights, but I didn't care about changing now. I was just so hungry. I got straight out of bed and went downstairs and had a pile of toast and some juice and then grabbed some biscuits, a banana and my water bottle, and stuffed it all in my bag. Rachel had left early for work, and I was glad that I could just take what I wanted without her asking too many questions. I raided the back of the cupboard for chocolate and found some. Result. I was going to need it. Because when I'd woken up it had come to me – what I had to do. I'd skip school, just one more time, just this morning – school wouldn't expect to see me after yesterday anyway. I'd sort out a sick note later. I had to go to the library – see if I could find something about Catherine's death. Something in an old newspaper report. Something that might tell me more. Because the thought of talking to Frances again was just too hard. Talking to her had frightened me. She was old and ill and I didn't want to make her worse. I couldn't bear the thought that I might do that – upset her. Not again.

I picked my bag up off the table and slung it onto my back, ready to leave.

My phone rang in my pocket.

Rachel's work number.

"Hi," she said. "Did you get my note?"

"What note?"

"The one on the kitchen table, Ana."

"No…" I looked around for it, but I could see nothing.

"Never mind," she said. "How are you feeling?"

"Better," I said.

"Good. Did you eat this morning?"

"Yes. Just toast."

"Have you left the house yet?"

"I…" I didn't know what to say. Why was she asking me? Did she know I wasn't going to go in? That I had bunked yesterday? If she did, why wasn't she saying anything about it?

"Ana? Are you there?"

"Yes."

"So, have you left the house yet or not?"

"No, not yet," I said. "I'm – I'm just packing my bag now…"

"It's just I seem to have lost my phone. I thought I'd left

it at work, but it isn't here. Can you see it anywhere?"

"Where would it be?" I said.

"I don't know – try the hall."

I walked into the hall and moved the post and junk mail around searching.

"Why don't you ring it?"

I bent down to look under the side table.

"Got it – I've got it," I said, picking up the phone.

"Brilliant. Look, I'm expecting a call this afternoon. I'll come to school at lunchtime. How about I take you for a crêpe. You can give it to me then. Okay?"

I turned the phone over in my hand.

There was a missed call from school.

Yesterday. 3 p.m.

And a text saying voicemail had a new message.

"Ana? Did you hear me?"

"Yup. That's fine," I said.

"I'll meet you at the school gates. We'll walk to the crêperie together. Okay?"

"Okay," I said, and she hung up. I deleted the voicemail and the text message and turned her phone off, dropping it in my bag as I closed the front door behind me.

The local library was not like the school library. It smelled damp. It was muffled in every way; muffled noise, muffled people in muffled coats. It personified hush. The school library was bright and light, and full of computers.

I had no idea where to start. I went up to the desk and asked the librarian if she could help me. She sighed, set down her pen and said, "Come with me."

I followed her as she padded across the spongy carpet into a back room with three computers – well, sort-of-computer-looking machines. They looked like ancient relics.

"You've got your library number?"

I gave her Rachel's card. I'd taken it out of the kitchen drawer before I left. She plugged in the number across the card with her right hand, and pushed her glasses up over her nose with her left simultaneously.

"It's pretty simple. You put in some keywords…here… Use this scroll button here…to search through what comes up… Click into the record or report you wish to view. You can't take copies but you can make a note of the document number that comes up…here… And then you can always come back and go straight to it if you need to refer to it again." Every time she said the word "here" she pointed with a slightly arthritic finger, paused heavily and looked at me seriously through her smeary glasses.

When she left, I was relieved. I took my coat off, and started.

42 The Avenue.

Nothing. Of course. I wasn't sure why I'd plugged that in first.

I started again.

Drowning.

One hundred and thirty-six references came up in twenty-eight separate publications. I started to look through the first few. Nothing relevant. Anywhere the word "drowning" or "drown" occurred in any local newspaper or publication from the time records began seemed to be logged here.

The council offices are drowning in applications for…

Dog drowns after swimming in high river tides…

"*Drowned Rats*" was the caption under a photograph from 1967 of a group of pensioners who were all soaked by a new sprinkler system set up in a care home in Richmond.

I realized I could literally spend the next five days of my life in this room if I was going to get anywhere. I needed to narrow the search.

Catherine Wells, Drowning.

Typing it out, seeing her name like that in black and white, made it feel so real again. I could see her face opposite mine, the crowns of our heads gently touching as

I bent down to help her put on her shoes in the hall. Frances was laughing in the other room, and then she came out and she told us to hurry up so we could go out to play before it got dark. And we went. But I didn't want to go at all.

The computer churned through the records, and five publications came up from my search. The third report from the local newspaper – *The Teddington Times* dated Monday 28th September 1981 – told me all I needed to know:

Catherine Wells, aged six years, daughter of Frances and Alfred Wells (deceased), was found dead in the River Thames close to Teddington on Saturday 26th September. It is believed a member of the public discovered the child's body in the water at around 8.15 p.m. on Saturday evening, and immediately called the emergency services. Catherine Wells was pronounced dead at the riverside at 8.52 p.m.

Catherine was playing on the common land known locally as the Green in front of her home on The Avenue earlier that evening. She was playing with another child, who is believed to be a family friend. The child, who cannot be named for legal reasons, will continue to be questioned by police today. Her family, who were attending a party in the street at the time, were not available for comment.

Police have appealed for anyone who may have seen the two girls playing out on the Green, or by the Thames, on Saturday evening between the hours of 5.30 p.m. and 8.15 p.m., to come forward with information.

Detective Inspector Dyer of the Metropolitan Police, who is leading the investigation, said, "Catherine Wells was not reported missing on the day of her death, and it is therefore crucial to our investigation to ascertain exactly what happened to her between the hours of 5.30 p.m. and 8.15 p.m. when her body was discovered."

I must have read it five times, maybe ten. It was front page news, staring back at me in black and white. It wasn't some image or memory from inside my head. It was confirmation – in print. It was what had happened in my first life. And yet still, it gave me nothing of what I needed to know. It didn't tell me what I had done. I'd been playing on the Green. I remembered Frances telling us to go out and play. But a party? Being questioned by police? You'd have thought I would have remembered some or all of that. But I didn't.

I closed my eyes, to try and think.

All I could feel was guilt. I was covered in it, immersed; like standing in a pool of wet and sloppy algae, it clung on to me, and I could do nothing but cling on to it. And I saw the bows, the tartan bows, as they kept slipping in

Catherine's hair, sliding down from the top of her head until they were swinging around, nipping the back of her ears as she ran.

"We're going to the river, Catherine. We'll play hide-and-seek by the river."

That's what I'd said to her. Because I wanted her to go and hide so I didn't have to play with her any more. I wanted my dad. I wanted to play with my dad. I wanted him to come and play like he'd said he would. I didn't want Catherine. I wanted Catherine gone.

I went back into the main part of the library and found a free computer with internet access and started typing.

The Avenue, Teddington.

There it was. I could see it on the map. A stripe of black for the road, blue for the river and a strip of green for the Green in between. It was so close. I reckoned I could walk it easily from the library in under an hour.

I memorized the route.

"Find what you needed?" asked the librarian as I walked past the desk, like she was interested all of a sudden.

"Yes," I said as I walked through the heavy wooden doors out into the street. "Yes, I did."

I was going to The Avenue. I was going back to the place where it happened. I was going to see it. The Avenue. And I hoped that when I saw it, I might remember what I had done.

8.

I found The Avenue within forty minutes of leaving the library. I reckoned it was about an hour's walk from where I lived now with Rachel. It was absolutely mind-breaking to think that I lived so close to it. To think that out of the infinite number of places in this vast world, I had been born a second time, here again – so close to where I'd lived before.

I stood in the road looking at a row of twenty or so large red-bricked houses that stood opposite a piece of common land. This was the place I had remembered. The Avenue. I turned to look at the Green. There were trees and long grasses, and as I looked around me I swear I couldn't be completely sure whose life I was living.

I didn't move.

I could sense the water. The river. I looked over towards the willow trees on the other side of the Green. They all seemed to respond to my arrival, moving roughly in a sudden gust of cool wind. I pulled my arms into myself.

I was frightened. Why was I here? Why was this happening to me?

I stepped onto the grass, walked over to an old oak tree and leaned against it. I recognized the raised and battered roots at my feet. I'd jumped over them time and time again; I'd run around them – they were as familiar to me as an old pair of shoes.

I looked at the houses again.

I couldn't see the numbers on the houses.

I started to walk across the Green towards the road so I could see the houses and their numbers. I was looking for Frances's house. For number 42.

And then I saw it. The patterned tile, the red numbers. The swirls and curls. 42. It was just as I'd remembered it. Had nothing changed? Was it all as it had been before, when I had done something so wrong – here, in this exact place? There had to be a reason why I was here again. There had to be a reason.

My phone rang.

It made me jump.

It wasn't a number I knew.

I answered anyway.

"Where are you?" Rachel's voice was short and urgent. "I'm at the crêperie. They've let me use their phone. I couldn't find you outside school."

I looked at my watch. It was 12.40 p.m.

"On my way..." I said.

"Don't be long."

"Ten minutes," I said, and I started to run.

When I got to the crêperie I was completely out of breath. Rachel was sat at a table looking at the menu, which was pretty pointless because she always had the same thing – ham and cheese. I stood outside for a moment with my hand on the door to try and still my breath a little before I stepped inside.

"Hi!" I sat down.

"Have a look, see what you want to have," Rachel said, pushing the menu towards me. She didn't smile. I could tell she was cross. I was so late.

"So, what are you going to have?" Rachel asked.

"Not sure. I'm just looking."

"Have you got the phone?"

"Oh, yes," I said, leaning down to grab my bag off the floor.

I passed it to her. "Battery was low so I turned it off." It struck me I should have checked the phone again before handing it over. Too late.

"Okay," she said. "I'll order. What will you have?"

"Chocolate and caramel."

"For lunch?" she said, smiling. "Well, okay. Just this once."

She looked down, turned her phone on and took it with her to the counter.

I looked around. Loads of the kids from school came here. Jamie too. I scanned the room to see if he was here. He wasn't. But when I thought about the fact that he might walk in at any minute I felt nervous. Good nervous. When I looked over at Rachel and saw she was on her phone I felt nervous too, in a totally different way.

"So how was your morning?" Rachel said, coming back to the table with the crêpes and two big mugs of tea on a tray. Her voice was flat, her eyes were wide, open, searching me.

"Fine."

"School okay?"

"I…"

"You haven't been in!" she said, holding her phone up. "I've just picked up a message from the school. Apparently they left me a message yesterday too? You walked out of maths yesterday morning and you haven't been in school since. You lied to me, Ana," she said. "I can't believe you did that! Where have you been?"

"I was sick. I'm fine now," I said. I didn't feel fine now, but I couldn't tell her that. I had to pretend.

"Sick because you bunked school and you thought I'd find out, or actually sick?"

"I was sick, yesterday…you know that—" I could

hardly get a word in among hers.

"The school said you left before lunch. That you went to the toilets and never came back to class."

"I forgot to sign out. I just needed to—"

"And today? Where have you been today? I can't believe you've done this, Ana. It's so unlike you. What's going on?"

"Look…it's nothing. I'm okay—"

"What if something happened to you? No one knew where you were!"

"I'm sorry," I said, fixing my eyes on the table. "I'm sorry, okay?" I didn't say it like I meant it, but I did say it. And when she didn't come straight back at me, I looked up. Her eyes were red and wet and she was squeezing a paper napkin from the table into the palm of her hand. It was screwed up into a tight ball. She was trying not to cry. She was mad with me. She was right to be mad with me. And there was something in her anger and distress that was familiar – too familiar – and I knew that I didn't want to make her feel like this.

I reached over and grabbed her hand.

"I've been stupid. I'm sorry."

She took her hand back and straightened out the napkin, smoothing it flat on the table between us. She sighed before she spoke again.

"Grillie called last night," she said.

"How is she?" I asked, relieved at the change of subject.

"She's fine, but she wanted me to talk to you because she's had a call from someone called Frances Wells."

I picked up my tea and nodded. I tried to hide behind the mug. I could feel myself getting hotter, my face turning red.

"Apparently you went to see this Frances Wells? At the hospital?"

"Yes," I said. "I did."

"Can I ask why you did that?"

I went to open my mouth, but I didn't know what to say.

"It's just that this woman said to Grillie that your visit rather upset her."

"So, Frances – she talked to Grillie?" I said.

"Yes. They'd swapped numbers at the hospital, so they could play bridge."

"I didn't realize—"

"What?"

"That they were in touch."

"Does it matter, Ana?"

I didn't want Grillie talking to Frances. I didn't want Grillie to know about me. I didn't want Rachel to know anything. They couldn't know. Panic started to course through me, fast, like rapids over rocks.

"Why did you visit her in hospital, Ana? What's going on?"

I couldn't think of anything to say.

"What did you say to her, Ana?"

"I saw her – when I went to visit Grillie," I said. "And she seemed lonely and – I don't know – Grillie said she didn't have any visitors—"

"You went and asked her about her dead daughter?" Rachel said.

My ears started to make a rushing sound, like I was going to faint. I looked at the table and held on to it, to steady myself. I was hot. All over. I thought I might break into a sweat, and the rushing was still rising in my ears.

"I didn't mean to upset her," I whispered. "I'm sorry I did that. Really. I am."

"What's going on with you at the moment, Ana? Walking out of school, visiting people you don't know, old women who've had enough upset in their lives without you quizzing them about it all. I just don't get it. It worries me, Ana. What's going on?" Rachel's face was so close to me now, her whole body leaned forwards towards me across the table like she was begging me for an answer, and her words kept coming, questioning me, asking me for answers. But I had none. Her eyes were so small with the worry and the tears but I couldn't answer her – I had no answers.

"You wouldn't understand!" I said. I didn't mean to say it quite like I did, or so loud, and I pushed back my chair so that I could leave. It fell back and hit the floor with an almighty smack. The room went quiet.

I stood there for a moment, just looking at Rachel.

And then I walked out, and as I walked up the street, the air began to cool my face, and all I could think about was how Rachel didn't know anything about me. She thought she did, but she didn't. She didn't know anything at all. Not one single little thing.

9.

I went into school after I left the crêperie, but only because I had to. I didn't know whether Rachel would back me up with a sick note or whether she'd let me face the school sanctions, but either way I knew I just had to go in.

As I crossed the courtyard to go to registration I felt a hand on my rucksack, pulling me back. I turned round to see who it was.

"Hey, Ana!"

It was Jamie.

I couldn't stop myself smiling when I saw him. How did just seeing him make me do that? I felt instantly better.

"Are you okay?"

"Yeah. Thanks."

"Good," he said. "Because I was going to ask if you're around this weekend. Zak's parents are away. He's having a gathering…"

"A gathering?"

"Yeah – he doesn't want to call it a party otherwise word will get round."

"Okay."

"So I'll call you and maybe we can go – you and me – to Zak's. Or do something."

The thought of Jamie kissing me flittered through my mind quickly like a bird caught in flight on the wind. I was lifted warmly with the idea of it.

"Ana?" he said.

I opened my mouth to speak, but I didn't get the words out quick enough.

"Well, just think about it, yeah?" Jamie said to fill the pause, and suddenly he looked embarrassed, awkward. I knew it was a big thing that he'd asked, and I'd messed up. I'd totally messed up.

He walked away, taking out his phone and his tangled mass of headphones, leaving me standing in the courtyard alone as everyone else walked by to head in for registration. I watched him go among the crowd until he disappeared completely out of sight, and I wondered then whether the feeling I had in that moment of his going – the push and pull of it: the joy of his asking and the despair that I'd messed up – was something like the beginning of love.

* * *

I made it through the afternoon, but only just. All I wanted to do was sleep. To get back into my bed and curl up like I'd done the night before. To shut out the world. I didn't take my eyes off the clock the whole way through history, and when the bell went for the end of the day all I felt was relief.

I stood up, stuffed my books in my bag and headed out.

I didn't want to go home yet. I couldn't. I'd have to face Rachel, and apologize for the way I'd spoken to her in the crêperie. I knew I owed her an explanation, but I didn't know what I would say. So I just kept walking. I wasn't sure exactly where I was going, I just had to get away from school, from home, from Jamie. I didn't want to see him now either. I'd messed everything up. I'd have to text him and find a way to make it okay again. The thing was I really wanted to go to Zak's gathering on Saturday, but I wasn't sure that Rachel would let me after today. I couldn't ask her until I'd made things better with her. I had to make things better. And then I'd tell Jamie I could go with him to the party. I kept walking. I'd walked in the direction of The Avenue. I hadn't made any big decision to come. I just knew I wanted to see it again, to see if something else came to me. And of course no one would be looking for me here. No one.

I turned into The Avenue and crossed the road in front of the houses and walked onto the Green. I sat down on the tree roots of the old oak and took a sip from my water bottle. I knew I'd tripped over these roots before. I remembered a deep graze on my knee like a burn that wouldn't bleed. It wept yellow liquid before it eventually turned red and scabbed over, leaving a scar.

Instinctively I reached down and rubbed my knee with my hands, for comfort. I had no scar. Because that was Emma's scar. *I am Ana now*, I said to myself. *I am Ana*.

I looked up at the house again. 42. I remembered it so well. But what use was this? What use was it coming here – seeing and remembering this house?

I began to feel sick. I shook my head and stretched my arms up above it so I could take a bigger breath, make the sickness go away.

I could hear ducks, buggy wheels, the sniff and snuffle of the odd dog padding around the trees behind me. The river. The noise of the towpath too. Runners. Cyclists. It was busy. I didn't remember these sounds before. It felt like Catherine and I were the only ones there, on the Green, that evening. My memories were all silent. Except for me, and what I said:

"We're going to the river, Catherine. We'll play hide-and-seek by the river."

Those words just wouldn't go away.

"If you don't play I'll tell on you. You have to come or that's what I'll do."

I'd said that because I had to make her come. It was the only way to make her come.

And then I saw it. An ambulance. It was driving slowly along The Avenue right in front of me. I looked around to reassure myself that I was still here, where I thought I was, that this was actually happening, that it wasn't some new and crooked memory. I took another sip of water and swallowed hard. Yes, I was still here. The water was cold as it slipped down my throat.

The ambulance doors swung open and the ramp hit the road. The noise shot a jolt through my bones that made me judder and I folded my arms around myself instinctively for protection. There she was. Frances Wells. Old, but strong. She was being pushed in a wheelchair down the ambulance ramp and along the street. She was holding her front-door key in her hand and her bag was sat high on her lap. I couldn't move. I was transfixed. This was an almost-regal parade – Frances shrouded in a red blanket, the ambulance men processing in green – and as I watched them, I walked across the Green, towards number 42, my feet utterly in time with theirs.

I stopped.

I waited so I could watch them go inside.

But they didn't.

They kept on walking.

Further up the street, beyond 42… I started to run back

towards the trees on the Green, away from the houses, like a wild animal shunned. I looked back. Where were they going? She lived at 42. Frances Wells. 42 The Avenue. It had always been that way…hadn't it? That's what I had in my head after I saw her. 42 The Avenue. I had been so sure.

And then I saw it – the wall – as they walked up the pathway of 38 The Avenue. Rough brown stones. Blocks with symmetrical holes cut out of each brick, each hole shaped like a petal, each brick as rough and ugly as the next. I'd crouched down behind this wall. I'd hidden here. I'd traced the pebble-dash with my fingers and I'd grazed my knuckles while I'd waited. But what was I waiting for? Catherine was at the river. It was too late for her to find me now. I knew that. I knew she'd never find me now. Because I'd left her at the river.

10.

I went home, washed, changed my clothes. I must have checked my phone at least ten times, hoping for a message from Jamie. I owed him a call or a text, but still, I hoped that there might be something from him. There was nothing.

I went downstairs.

"You look better," Rachel said as I walked into the kitchen.

"Yeah – I feel it," I said, putting down my phone. I wasn't sure if we were okay now. We hadn't talked since lunchtime. Really, I owed her an apology. But when we'd had rows before Rachel usually let them drift, pretend like nothing had happened. It suited me now to do that too.

"Do you want this crêpe then?" Rachel said, pointing at a doggy bag on the table.

"Yeah," I said. "Thanks." And I opened up the bag, lifted the crêpe out of its box and started eating. I was relieved. It seemed like things were okay.

"Is it nice?" she said.

I nodded. But it wasn't. It was cold and it was sticking to the back of my throat. I felt sick. But I had to keep up the act. And I still needed to ask her about a letter for school explaining my absence. And Zak's party.

I forced myself to take another bite.

I gagged.

Rachel saw me.

"Ana!"

I stood up, walked over to the sink and spat the contents of my mouth into it.

"What are you doing?"

"I can't eat it," I said. "I thought I was going to be sick."

"Sit down. Have some water."

I sat back down at the table, and Rachel brought the water over and sat next to me. I took a couple of sips and neither of us spoke for a minute or two.

"Can I ask you something?" I said.

"Of course."

"Have I ever mentioned the name…Catherine… before?"

Saying her name, out loud, like that, to Rachel, it felt somehow wrong. Like I was giving away my biggest secret, but I had to ask.

"You had an imaginary friend for a bit. I think you were about four or five at the time. She was called Catherine."

"Catherine?" I said. "Are you sure?"

"Yes. I don't know where you got the name from. Maybe a book, or TV. There weren't any Catherines around at the time."

"So what did I used to say…about Catherine?"

"Oh, I don't remember…" she said.

"You must remember something?"

"Actually, yes – you played hide-and-seek a lot. I remember that now. It was always hide-and-seek."

She stood up and went over to the sink.

"Why are you asking?" she said, over her shoulder.

"Oh, nothing. Just wondering…about the name… I don't know…"

"Right."

"I think I'll have an early night, Rachel," I said.

"Okay. Call down if you need anything," she said.

I took myself up to bed and slid under the duvet again in all my clothes. I closed my eyes, but sleep just wouldn't come. Because all I could see was Catherine in the water. Her hair splayed out and her head motionless as she lay in the darkness of the river, her eyes wide open as if she too could see the horror of what I had done. Had I known about Catherine – had I known but never allowed myself to think about her? Had I blocked out Catherine and what happened to her because it was just too awful to face?

I stared at the ceiling while the hours passed and I waited. I waited for the light to return so that I could get up and go straight back to The Avenue. It was the only thing I could think to do.

friday

11.

I took Rachel a cup of tea in bed at seven o'clock and told her I had to be in early for auditions for the school play, that I'd forgotten to tell her last night, that I'd see her later. She nodded and gladly took the tea.

And I took the bus and went straight to The Avenue and stood on the Green by the trees. They hid me and I wanted them to. I didn't want anyone to see that I was here. I might have been wrong about Frances's house number, but not about Catherine. We'd played hide-and-seek. I'd wanted my dad to myself. I'd taken her to the river and told her to go and hide, and it was dark, and she'd died because I'd killed her. I might have played with Catherine in this life as if she were my imaginary friend, but she was real. She was Frances's daughter, and she had lived and she had died, and it was because of me.

I looked up at number 38.

I stood and I looked at it.

I felt an urge to go inside.

But why? To do what? To see Frances again? Frances was old, and she was ill, and how could I go to her after what I had done? I couldn't. Except she was the only person in all the world I could talk to now. The only one.

My heart started to pulse in my chest.

I looked around.

I was frightened.

I wanted Mum.

I wondered whether I'd ever find her.

Ever see her again.

If I was here, living a second life to face the horror of what I had done, if I had to pay for it in some way, then I'd do that – I'd face it, I'd pay. But I needed my mum. I needed her.

Dry grief grazed my throat raw. I felt so full of feeling and yet so empty. Since seeing Frances, nothing was normal any more. Normal life had been replaced by huge swathes of emotion. The fear of what I'd done and the longing always for my mum was twisting tighter and tighter around me all the time now. It was suffocating me, and there was nothing I could do.

I stepped out from under the trees and started walking towards the houses. Putting one foot in front of the other grounded me.

I should go. I should go to school.

I took a deep breath and looked up again.

And that's when I saw her.

Frances.

She was stood at her front door, and she was beckoning me over.

I went towards her.

"It's you," she said, when I reached the front path. "I've been watching you."

I didn't answer.

"You know I have very little else to do these days but look out at the world from here."

There was silence.

"Did you come to see me?" she said.

I nodded. I hadn't thought that I had, but she was right. I had.

My throat was still so dry.

I wasn't sure whether my voice would be there if I tried to speak.

I swallowed.

"Come in," Frances said.

I didn't reply.

Suddenly I felt unsure about going inside.

Frances looked at me.

"You know, you never told me your name," she said.

"Ana," I said. "It's Ana."

"That's right," she said. "I did know that. Millie told me. Ana what?"

"Ana Ross," I said.

"Well, Ana Ross. I think you should come in." And she opened the door wider to let me through.

And I went.

Because in that moment I knew I had no choice but to do exactly as Frances said.

12.

Frances indicated for me to go into the front room. The windows were vast, the curtains were heavy. I saw her young. Her slim waist, her navy dress. I heard the muted laughter. It was all with me again in an instant. I felt uncomfortable in this room. I had wanted my dad here. An overwhelming need for him came over me. For a moment I thought I might cry the tears I had cried as a child, when I had needed him then.

"Please, sit down." Frances pointed to a chair. "Do you want tea?"

"No, I'm fine," I said. I looked at my watch. It was still early, but I'd need to start making my way to school really soon. "I won't stay long."

"Good," Frances said, sitting down in an armchair. She looked like she was in pain, as she sat.

"I didn't mean to upset you when I came to the hospital," I said. "I really didn't mean to—"

"I was surprised you knew her name," Frances cut in.

"Catherine's name." And as she spoke she looked me directly in the eye in a way that made me feel so uneasy.

"I…I came to the hospital because—"

"I may be old," she interrupted, "but I'm certain we have never met before, Ana."

It felt wrong, her saying my name the way she did.

So I just said it.

The words that had been going round and round in my head.

"I'm Emma," I said. "I'm Emma Trees." And as I said it, I felt as if a sweet warm wind had blown across my face and it bathed me, all of me.

Frances sat utterly still. "You can't be Emma."

"I know it seems impossible, but—"

"You said you were Ana."

"And I am Ana – now—"

"Emma Trees died."

"I know," I said.

"Emma Trees is dead," she said again. "She died thirteen years after Catherine. If you know that, then you know you cannot be her."

"I was playing, with Catherine—"

"Emma was twenty-two, she was twenty-two, and you – you're—"

"We were playing, on the Green, out the front – here—"

"You can't be more than sixteen—"

"We were on the Green, and—"

We were both speaking fast, we were both listening to each other but desperately clinging to what we knew. Frances took a short breath, and neither of us spoke for a minute.

"Everyone knew Catherine was on the Green before she died," she said. "It doesn't make you Emma Trees."

"But I was there. I remember it. I was with her..." The desperation in my voice was back.

"I think you must be mistaken," she said.

I looked at her and as I did all I could see was Catherine's pretty face looking back at me. Mother and daughter, they had the same almond-shaped eyes.

"I fixed her hair clips," I said. "The tartan bows."

Frances looked at me.

"They matched her skirt," I said. "The bows. She was dressed for a party. White tights and black patent shoes with buckles. I did them up for her, here, in the hall. The hair clips wouldn't stay in. She said she didn't want to wear them, but she—"

"I made her wear them," Frances said. "For the party."

We sat in silence for a moment. I didn't know where to look any more. If I looked away and looked back at her my eyelids started flickering, blinking with nervousness, fear. I felt like I shouldn't say any more but I wanted – needed – to carry on, to tell Frances what I knew.

"Tell me something else," Frances said. "Something you think you know about Catherine, about that night."

"We were playing ball. On the Green," I said. I could see the ball now. It came back to me. "We had a blue ball. You wiped it clean before we played with it. You got the ball out of the shed and you wiped it clean in the kitchen..." I pointed through to where the kitchen was, desperate to show her what I knew. "Through there."

"Go on," she said.

"You tried to wipe the ball with a wet cloth and the dirt smeared across the ball, across your hands," I said. "You were angry, with the mess. You went to a drawer and got a dry tea towel and you wiped it clean and told us to go out onto the Green and play. I think—"

Frances raised her left hand. She wanted me to stop talking. I stopped at her command. I looked at her, waiting for her to allow me to carry on, to keep talking. She was utterly still.

"Why are you here?" she said.

"I need to know what happened. I need to know how she died."

"You don't remember?" Frances said, her voice rising steadily, but with the utmost control. "You don't remember what you did?"

I shook my head.

"You're lucky," she said.

"Why?"

"Don't ask me that!" she barked back. "You can't ask me that!"

There was silence.

And then she spoke again. "Why did you come here?" she said.

"The answers – they're here. They must be."

"Why?"

"You, Catherine, this house, that night... It's all here. Isn't it? We were here—"

"How long have you known?" Frances interrupted.

"That I'm Emma?" I said.

Frances nodded.

"I've always known that I'm Emma," I said. "But I hadn't remembered about Catherine. Not until this week. Not until I saw you in the hospital. We were there, weren't we? Both of us, that night?" I said. "I...I just had to speak to you. Since I saw you in the hospital I've been remembering things, things I haven't remembered before. I have no one else to talk to. There is no one I can tell."

Frances continued to look at me. She was searching me with her eyes, and even though I didn't like it – how it made me feel – I let her, because I was desperate for her to let me stay and talk.

"I don't know why I should believe you," she said.

"Because you have to!" I said, my voice getting louder.

"Because there is no explanation for what I know—"

"There are no explanations," Frances said. "None! I've been searching for an explanation. I've been waiting for a reason, an understanding, an answer as to why she died. I've been asking for a sign, for something – anything – to come to me through every day of every one of the long, long years since she died. And there has been nothing."

"Maybe I know things you don't...?" I said.

"I doubt that," she said.

"I have memories, images, inside my head—"

"I have those too, Ana."

"But they won't be the same. I was with her, wasn't I? Before she died?"

"You were," Frances said, slowly, looking at me again. "So you remember that?"

I nodded.

"Would you talk to me?" I said. "Please. Could you do that?"

There was another silence between us.

"We aren't the same – you and I," Frances said. "What you did sets you apart. If I agree to talk, you must never forget that." And she looked at me in a way that made me cold, all over. I could feel my skin rippling with the chill.

I shivered. And I opened my mouth to speak—

"What I want to know," she said, "is why you are here."

I shook my head. "I don't know."

"So what *do* you know? It seems to me the answer is not very much, young Ana."

"I need you, Frances. To help me," I cried.

"Ah!" she said. "Help!" And her voice was getting louder now. "Where was *my* help when I needed it?"

"Maybe…maybe," I said, stuttering, "maybe it's me? Maybe I'm here, now, to help, to help you…to help you understand…"

Could it be that I'd come back to make things better? I didn't know, but I grasped on to any reason I could find if it meant that Frances would keep talking to me.

"But you can't change what happened, can you? You might have come back, Ana – Emma – whoever you are. But Catherine. She's never coming back. Is she?" Her voice was low, controlled, challenging me.

"No," I said, quietly. "I don't think so."

"Nothing will bring my Catherine back," she said, her voice rising again, angry. "Don't you see? Nothing! And yet you – you are here."

"I know," I said. "I'm sorry." I could feel tears, welling in my throat.

"There must be a reason!" she said again. "I want a reason!"

"I – I can't explain it," I said. "I – I just feel so bad – I…" And the black, black feeling was rising up inside me.

It filled me up – all of me – and the tears came – heavy. I thought they would never stop.

"You should try!" Frances shouted, standing up awkwardly from her chair to look out of the window. "You should at least try after what you did!"

I stood up, unsure of what to do. Frances had turned her back on me.

I took in a breath. I wasn't sure whether I should just leave, but I was suddenly too frightened to move.

"If I had anything left to lose – anything at all – I would be asking you to leave," Frances said. "But I don't."

And then she turned around to face me. "I'll talk to you, Ana," she said. "But don't ask me to forgive you for what you did. Don't ever ask me to do that."

"I understand," I said. "I understand."

And I said it twice, because I did.

"Hi! I'm back!" Rachel called out as she got in from work later that day. "How were the auditions?"

"Good, yeah," I said.

I hadn't made it in for registration. I'd got a late. I wasn't going to tell her that now.

"Do you think you'll get a part?" Rachel asked, walking into the kitchen. I was making myself a snack.

"Maybe," I said, opening up the bread bin. "Are you

okay to give me a sick note, by the way?"

I turned my back on Rachel as I spoke, trying to avoid looking her in the face. I knew I was pushing my luck by asking for the note, but I just had to.

"Okay," she said. "This time. But please, no bunking off again. There are no second chances if you bunk off again. Do you understand?"

"Yeah," I said, and I started buttering the bread. I was hungry.

"You've got your appetite back, I see."

"Yeah," I said. "I'll just have a sandwich now, if that's all right?"

"Fine. I'll cook us something a bit later." She paused. "Glad you're feeling better."

My phone beeped with a text.

"Rachel?" I said, turning to face her. "There's a gathering on Saturday night. At Zak's. Can I go?"

"Sure," she said. "But I don't want you out late. I'll pick you up. Before eleven. If you can cope with that, then yes, you can go."

"Thanks," I said, picking up my phone.

"Well, I think I'll go up and have a bath," she said. She paused for a moment in the doorway of the kitchen before she spoke again. "I love you, you know," she said.

"I know," I said, but still, I was looking at my phone.

"And one day you'll actually look at me and tell me

you love me too, Ana Ross. Because I know that you do," she said.

I looked up at her, still smiling, and Rachel smiled back, like she always did. Except today I wasn't sure whether behind the smile there was a sadness.

But I didn't want to think about that. Not now.

I looked down at my phone again.

A text from Jamie.

Zak's gathering is on. Will you come? J x

I texted back straight away.

Yes. I'll be there. A x

And suddenly the world felt full of possibility, and all the sickness and the sadness I'd been feeling had dulled. It was almost gone.

saturday

13.

The gathering was most definitely a party. It didn't matter what Zak wanted to call it. There must have been forty or fifty people standing around in the house – up the stairs, in the halls, hanging out, drinking cans. The music was loud as we walked in and there were loads of people I didn't know, so I just followed Jamie. I could see he was checking out all the rooms, and who was there, until eventually we headed out the back door and into the garden, where there were people smoking and chatting. Zak had his guitar out and was strumming some vaguely recognizable tune. Hannah was sat down next to him. She had her arm resting on his leg as he played and kept looking up at him adoringly. They looked so good together. I wondered whether me and Jamie would ever look like that. Jamie's hand suddenly clasped mine, and he was pulling me over to sit with Zak and Hannah and the others. Someone passed me a can, and I opened it up. Cider. Hannah smiled at me and nodded at Jamie, and it was clear she and Zak were the king and queen of this little gathering by the back door.

"Cool party," said Jamie.

Zak nodded. "Glad you could make it, mate. All right, Ana?"

"Yeah," I said and I nodded, letting the cider slip down my throat. The sweetness on my tongue almost tingled, and the more I sipped, the warmer and sweeter I felt.

Zak carried on playing, and people kept joining and leaving our crowd but Hannah stayed exactly where she was, and me and Jamie did the same. I felt safe here in the garden, next to Jamie. The rest of the party wasn't making much sense to me. I hadn't been to loads of parties. I wasn't sure they were my thing. It felt good being with Jamie, but I felt separate from everything else that was going on. Occasionally I'd look into the house. People just seemed to be endlessly milling about, dancing, laughing, talking, occasionally jibing each other but only to then have a laugh about it, and the longer I sat there, and the louder it got, the more separate I felt. I kept thinking about what Frances had said to me yesterday: "Nothing will bring my Catherine back," she'd said. "And yet you – you are here… There must be a reason…"

She was right.

Here I was, back in the world, again, and yet the more I thought about it, the less sense it made. Why was I here?

It was Catherine who deserved a second life. Not me.

I felt myself leaning into Jamie. He was sat just behind me. When I turned around to say something to him his face was right there, close to mine. I could feel myself letting go, allowing myself to be drawn into him, the warmth of him, the solidness.

"Are you cold?" Jamie asked.

"A bit," I said.

"Come on, let's go inside."

He took my hand again and led me back into the house, grabbing a bottle of cider that was sitting by the kitchen sink. He turned and winked at me as he took it and I giggled, like a child, which surprised me. And I liked him holding my hand. I liked it a lot.

We snaked our way through people dancing in the front room. I was glad Jamie didn't want to dance. George and Jessie were kissing at the top of the stairs. We stepped over them as we went. They didn't even seem to notice we were there. Someone must have been taking an age in the loo and a couple of girls I recognized from school were calling out and banging on the door. Jamie led me up to Zak's room in the loft. It was much quieter up there. I could hardly make my way across the floor for the mess, but it was quiet, and suddenly we were alone.

"Did you want to dance?" he said, letting go of my hand and walking over towards the TV.

"No," I said, looking around. I wasn't sure what to do, where to sit.

Billy was passed out over a sofa bed on one side of the room, lying on his front with his mouth wide open.

"Look who's here!" I whispered, looking over at Jamie for his reaction.

"He always peaks too early," Jamie said, messing about with the TV. "Do you want to watch something?"

"What's Zak got?" I asked.

I wasn't sure I really wanted to start watching a film but I grabbed a couple of beanbags anyway and slid myself into a vaguely comfortable position, kicking all Zak's clothes and shoes out of the way.

"Let's try this," he said, grabbing the remote and lying down next to me on the floor.

As soon as the movie started I felt like my senses were on overload; my whole body felt charged by the possibility that Jamie and I might actually touch. Jamie sighed and started to move around, to get comfortable. He was getting closer, shifting himself onto the beanbag next to me. And then I heard footsteps on the stairs. Zak and Hannah walked in. Hannah could hardly walk straight and she was holding Zak's hand and giggling.

"What are you watching?" Zak asked, sitting down.

"Shhh," said Jamie. "It's started."

I smiled at Hannah and she giggled and looked at me

and mouthed, "Sorry to crash your party." And as she did she slipped down to the floor next to Zak like a puppet coming off its strings.

Jamie and I moved closer into each other again to make room for them and Jamie tilted his head to one side, towards me. I knew I wanted to kiss him. I knew in that instant that I wanted to take his head gently in my hands and lift his lips to mine and kiss him, like I'd kissed someone before, when I was Emma. But I couldn't do it. I couldn't do it because Zak and Hannah and Billy were there and I was scared. Emma wouldn't have been scared. I was sure of that. But I was. And then Frances's words were with me again: "Nothing will bring my Catherine back. And yet you – you are here… There must be a reason."

I sipped some more cider. I took three or four smooth sips. I wanted more of that warmth, and the slowness it brought. I looked at the screen in front of me. Did I not have a right to be here? I didn't ask to be born again. I didn't will it to happen. Me being here again, living my second life, this was just the way it was, the way it had always been. I turned my head to look at Jamie. I wanted to reassure myself that he was still there, right there, next to me. All of him next to all of me. And I closed my eyes. And I wished for a moment where none of it mattered.

"Are you okay?" Jamie whispered.

I opened my eyes to him.

"Ana…" he said, and he lifted his hand up and stroked my cheek as he said it.

Surely I had a right to be here.

Surely I had every right in the world.

sunday

14.

"How are you feeling?" Rachel asked as soon as I walked into the kitchen the next morning.

"Okay," I said.

"Tea?"

I nodded.

My phone buzzed.

A text.

Great to see you last night. J x

I smiled as I remembered how we'd laid down next to each other at the party. It'd felt so good to be close to him like that. And I smiled too when I remembered how he had looked at me when he stroked my cheek.

Rachel handed me my tea. I took a gulp. It was hot and sweet. Just what I needed.

"Did you drink last night, Ana?"

"Just one," I said. "Maybe two." I actually didn't know

how much I'd had. My head did hurt a little this morning.

"I worry when I think about you drinking too much," Rachel said.

"I didn't drink too much," I said. "It was only cider anyway."

"It's still alcohol. You know the rules. You look terrible. And I'm not here today, did you remember? I've got to go into work to pack up for the office move."

"I'll be fine. Don't worry," I said.

I hadn't remembered Rachel would be out.

"So have you got plans?"

"I don't know, but I'll be fine," I said, and as I said it I thought about The Avenue. I could go back to The Avenue. Talk to Frances again.

"Well, look, I think you should just stay here and take it easy. You've got homework anyway, and I guess there's stuff you need to catch up on from last week?"

I nodded.

"I'll be as quick as I can," she said, and she drained her cup and put it in the sink. "Call me," she said. "Later."

"Sure," I said, but in my head I was already halfway to Teddington, my mind bursting with the things I could talk to Frances about.

15.

“There was a party. Do you remember?” Frances said, as we sat down in the sitting room.

I’d got to The Avenue by eleven and Frances seemed almost pleased to see me when she’d opened the front door.

“No,” I said. “I don’t remember a party, but I knew Catherine was dressed for a party. Was it a birthday?”

“No,” Frances said. “There was a party at number 50 every September. It was an annual thing. The Williamses put it on. It was drinks – friends and neighbours. It wasn’t a children’s party.”

“I didn’t want to go,” I said. It came to me. “I remember saying to Dad that it would be boring. He promised he’d play with me on the Green before the party. He said he’d make it fun, and I believed him.” And I could feel, as I said it, how much I hadn’t wanted to go to the party, and how much I didn’t want to have to play with Catherine and how much he’d let me down when he hadn’t come and played with me on the Green.

Frances looked at her fingers. They were clasped together in her hands. She was utterly composed. I knew what she was thinking. That she wished I hadn't come to play with Catherine. Because maybe then none of this would have happened. Catherine would still be alive today.

"The evening might have been many things," Frances said, "but I don't think you could have said it was boring."

"I'm sorry."

She nodded.

"They should have left me at home," I said. I was trying to make better what I had said.

"They couldn't have done that, Ana. Someone would have had to look after you. Amanda, your mum, couldn't find anyone to babysit that night."

"They could have left me at home with a friend or a neighbour, couldn't they?"

"That was the problem. Everyone was invited to the party, Ana!" Frances said.

I looked at her blankly. "What do you mean, *everyone*?"

"You don't remember?" Frances said.

"I…"

I felt panicked now. A vague sickness began to shift and rise in my belly.

"You lived here, Ana. 42 The Avenue," she said. "This street was your home."

My ears started filling with air, and the familiar sickness rose – it was in my throat now. I thought I might pass out…the tiles, the pathway, the house. It was mine. It was where I had lived. 42 The Avenue. Emma's home. It was mine.

"You were born here," she said. "I'm sure you would have lived here your whole life, but Amanda, well, she said that after what happened, the family couldn't stay. That you had to move – in order to 'move on', is what she said."

Frances's words were fast. My brain was scrambling them, trying to hold them all together, to make sense of them, to understand.

And suddenly I could see Mum screaming. I could see her pretty face filled with red rage and she was screaming over and over – "*How did this happen! How?*" Dad was there too – standing, motionless – and they were looking at me. They were both looking at me with a mixture of pity and pain in their eyes. "*How could you have done this? How could you?*" Mum had screamed.

"Richard was a good man," Frances said.

My dad. She was talking about my dad.

"And Mum?" I asked.

I wanted to know about my mum.

"Good enough," Frances said. Her words were long and slow.

"I wish they were here, now."

The words just came out of me, and I felt the lump in my throat again as I said them – a bundle of tears all wrapped up, holding tight to one another, so as not to spill.

"You mean Amanda and Richard?"

"Yes," I said. "I miss them." And as I said it my eyes filled with the tears, the bundle unravelling down my cheeks as I spoke. "I miss them so much."

"But you came back to *me*, Ana. Not to them. You came to *me*!" said Frances.

"It's just – I mean... Do you know where they are?" I tried to wipe the tears from my face, to stop them coming. "Do you know where they live?"

I saw Frances's lips tighten. Her whole mouth had tightened around the jaw. "I have an address," she said. "When they moved from here they moved out of London. To Berkshire. I have no idea whether they are still there."

"Can I have the address?" I asked, and as I did I could hear myself. I sounded like a spoilt, ungrateful child, angling for all the sweets in the jar. But I didn't care, not if it meant I might get to see them both again, my mum and my dad. But especially my mum. In that moment I would have done anything anyone asked of me if it meant I could see Mum again. If I could see Mum and she could make it all better. "Or if you don't want to give it to me," I said, and I grabbed a pen and an old receipt from my bag and started scribbling, "this is my mobile number and my address. You could give it to them?"

"You can have their address, Ana. If I can find it. It's in an old address book somewhere," she said. "I'll look for it. Another day." And she stood up awkwardly to take the receipt from me as I leaned forwards to pass it over and then we sat in silence for a moment as she struggled to sit back down.

"It's not so easy," she said. "Looking back. Is it?"

"No," I said, wiping my eyes again.

"I look back every day," she said. "For Catherine, for the answers as to why this happened."

She looked at me. Her stare was hard. I could feel the weight of her anger and sorrow pressing down on me. It was like a train moving slowly, steadily, heavily over my chest. Her pain felt like it was crushing me.

"I want to know why you did what you did. I want to know why you killed my daughter," she said.

"I—"

"You must realize that is the only reason I have let you into my home. So I can ask you and hear your answer – the answer I've been waiting for all this time."

"I'm so sorry," I said, and I started sobbing. "I'm so sorry." And I kept saying it because I didn't know what else to say.

"Hearing you say that," Frances said, "it means nothing

to me. I thought it might be worth something – to hear it, an apology – but it's not. And you know why, Ana? Because it changes nothing."

I looked up through my tears. Frances's face was hard, worn. There was nothing I could say to her. Nothing I could say to make any of it better.

"Does your mother know you are here, Ana?" she said.

"Rachel? No," I said.

"What does she know – about you?" Frances asked.

"Nothing," I said, shaking my head.

"And you don't want her to know?"

"She mustn't ever know," I said. "It would break her heart."

Frances nodded, and took a sip of tea from the cup that was sat in front of her on the table. Her fingers curled around the cup like the warped branches of a dead tree, and I could see that it hurt for her to move, to lift it to her mouth.

I watched her for a moment.

"Are you okay?" I asked.

She swallowed and put the cup back down on the table slowly.

I waited.

"Osteoarthritis, osteoporosis, and now gallstones," she said. "Bones are crumbling. Body's packing up. Not much I can do."

"Are you in pain?"

"Most of the time," she said.

"And today?"

"Today isn't such a good day. In fact, you could pass me my pills. They are in the sideboard," she said, pointing to the other side of the room.

I stood up and walked over towards the sideboard.

"Second drawer down," she said.

I opened the drawer and saw papers and pens, a pack of playing cards and a small plastic pill pot, all arranged neatly in the drawer. And there, to the right, was a stack of birthday cards. *You Are One* and *Two Today!* I flipped them between my hands inside the drawer. They were old, worn. My heart sped up. There were more underneath. *Congratulations! You are 3! 4! 5!* I turned around to see if Frances was looking over at me. She wasn't. She was filling a glass with water for her pills from a carafe on the table next to the tea. These were Catherine's cards. They had to be. I felt as if somebody had their hands around my neck. My throat was tight. There was no air. I glanced back at Frances again and then pulled in a deep and painful breath before opening one of the cards to read.

Dear Catherine,
Happy Birthday!
With love,

Amanda, Richard and Emma

This was Mum's writing. It was hers. I let my fingers stroke the card where her pen had been. I was close to her, in that moment, closer than I'd ever been before. I quickly opened another card, my hands still in the drawer.

Dear Catherine
Have a day filled with fun!
Lots of love,
Amanda, Richard and Emma

And still, another, the same.

From Amanda, Richard and Emma

And on one, I'd signed my own name.

Emma

And in another I'd drawn a smiley face –

For my friend Catherine ☺

My writing was big, scrawled.

"Can't you find them?" Frances asked. I jumped at her voice and then I took one of the cards and put it in my skirt pocket. It was instinctive. I just knew I had to have the card. To have something that had been touched and held by Mum.

"Got them," I said, holding the pill pot up to show Frances, and I closed the sideboard drawer.

I went and sat back down and passed over the pills. I watched while Frances opened the pot up and tipped the contents out into the palm of her hand. She was slow. So slow. Arranging and rearranging the pills on the table and then again in her hand. And as I waited I felt anxious, restless.

I looked out of the window at the Green.

And suddenly it was there. An almost-immediate pain – and with it that feeling again. My dad. I'd been waiting for him to come and play. Where had he been?

I turned back to Frances.

"He didn't come out and play," I said, and as I said it I felt as if I was still waiting for him now, willing him to come.

"What are you talking about?" Frances said, setting down her glass of water on the table in front of her.

"Dad. He never came out and played like he said he would. He never came."

"He was talking to me," said Frances.

"To you? But he was meant to come out and play

with *me*—" I said and I recognized the child in my voice as I did.

"I'm sure he would have come, but we had things we needed to talk about. What does it matter, Ana?" Frances said.

"It matters," I said. "To me!"

"Why?" Frances said.

"Where was Mum?"

"She was already at the party. You'd all gone to the party early – around half past five. Amanda was helping with the food. She'd baked. She was always baking something. So you and Richard helped Amanda carry the food over to the party and then he brought you over here to see Catherine. The plan was that the four of us would go to the party when it started at half past six. But none of this matters, Ana. None of it. Because it isn't what happened."

"We're going to the river, Catherine. We'll play hide-and-seek by the river."

"If you don't play I'll tell on you. You have to come or that's what I'll do."

"What were you and Dad talking about?" I asked.

"I don't remember," Frances said.

"But he never came," I said, again. "He'd promised!"

"You never could accept the way things were. Never! You could never just leave things alone! And still – now—"

"But you said you had things you needed to talk about

with Dad. That's what you just said. You must remember what those things were."

"I told you. I don't remember," Frances said.

I looked at Frances. She was lying. I knew she was. She was pretending she didn't know, because she didn't want to say.

Neither of us spoke for a moment.

"What have you got there?" she said, suddenly pointing her crooked finger at my pocket. I looked down. The card I'd taken was sticking out so it could be seen.

"Nothing," I said, tucking it back in.

"It's something of mine, isn't it?" Frances said. "From the sideboard. Show it to me!"

I didn't move.

"Now!" she said.

I pulled the card out of my pocket and held it in my hand. I didn't want to give it back to her, but Frances was shouting at me. She was shouting.

"That was Catherine's. Give it back to me!"

I stood up and put the card down on the table in front of her, just out of reach. It was cruel, I knew it was, but I didn't want to lose it.

"I can't reach it from there!" she said. "Put it here, in my hand." And as she held out her hand towards me I could see it was so weak. The only strength was in her voice, her words.

I didn't move.

"You stupid, stupid girl! Give it to me. Now!" she screamed.

"Don't shout at me!" I screamed back. "Don't shout at me like that!" And I heard in my voice a fury like I had never heard before.

"You don't understand anything!" Frances said. "You are just like Emma! Just like her! Now give me the card!"

"No!" I said, snatching it back off the table, taunting her with it. I knew it was childish, but I couldn't bear being shouted at like this – like I'd been shouted at before.

"She's dead! She's gone! Because of you! How could you? We trusted you and she's gone."

Frances's voice was in my head now – from before – shouting, screaming...she was crying—

"Get out! Get out of my house! Get her out! Now!"

She was raging – at me.

And there was nowhere I could hide.

I had nowhere to hide.

"Why have you still got these cards?" I said.

"They are my daughter's birthday cards, Ana!"

"But they're from us – from Mum and Dad and me." And I walked over to the sideboard, opened it again and began to pull out the cards. "There are only cards here from us – no one else! Catherine must have had cards from other people. Not just us!"

I walked back towards Frances.

She didn't speak.

"I want to know why you've kept these cards – only these. Our family's cards to Catherine. She must have had others!" I said. "Why would you keep cards from me after I did what I did to her?" And I saw her arm rise up from the chair in front of me, and the next thing I felt was a hot and scorching pain across my left cheek where Frances's pale and bony hand had struck me hard.

The card fell to the table, fluttering in the air as it went. I raised both my arms to defend myself against a second blow. I was sure another was coming. I closed my eyes and waited.

Nothing.

I opened my eyes.

Frances was sat back down in front of me. The card was now between the palms of her hands, her twisted fingers clasped around it so tightly all the blood had drained from under her nails. They were almost blue.

I will not cry. I will not cry. I will not cry.

That's what I said to myself as I stood there, trying to take in what had just happened, my cheek burning with the rising bruise.

And then I picked up my bag and I walked out. And as I went I glanced at Frances, and I swear she was smiling.

16.

No one told me that standing up high, and I mean really high – on-top-of-a-building Spiderman high, where all you can see is the sky, until there is no more sky to see – would make me feel okay. But then I don't know who could have told me that.

I am lucky.

Lucky that today – this afternoon, while Rachel was at work – I climbed out of my bedroom window and discovered that if I swung my leg around far enough to the right, I could lever myself up and make it onto the bathroom window ledge and then onto the flat roof.

I don't know what made me do it.

Well, maybe, thinking about it now, I do.

I needed to get away. Just for a little while. And there was literally nowhere else to go.

monday

17.

I didn't sleep.

I couldn't.

Being shouted at like that, being hit. It stayed with me.

I lay in bed, still, all night, with my eyes open, trying to feel blank. Trying to feel nothing. But my feelings were all over me, like itches I couldn't reach to scratch.

"Ana, sit down. I want to talk to you."

Rachel was stood in the kitchen waiting for me the next morning. She looked hassled. Worried. I sat at the table and pulled up my knees to hug them to me. I wasn't sure I could eat any breakfast. I'd grab something if I needed to on the way to school. I took a sip of juice. It was cold. Too cold. It made my teeth hurt. I touched my cheek. I hoped my make-up had covered the mark on my face. I didn't think Rachel had noticed the bruise last night. She'd gone out, and we'd talked when she got in, but I was in bed with just the side light on. I looked tired this morning. I knew that. I had bags under my eyes, but in a way that helped;

it masked the slight swelling on my cheek. There was no way I could have explained to Rachel what had happened yesterday. No way.

"You look tired. Did you sleep last night?"

"I'm fine," I said.

"Right, but are you sleeping?"

"I'm waking up a bit, during the night. It's nothing." I didn't want to tell her I was so exhausted I didn't know how I was going to get through the day.

"You cried out in your sleep last night. Did you realize?"

"No," I said. I wanted to change the subject.

"Are you having nightmares again?"

"Again?"

"You had them before—"

"When?"

"Years ago now," she said.

I shrugged, like it didn't matter, but I didn't remember having nightmares before, and it bothered me. I was sure I hadn't slept at all last night, but I must have done if I'd cried out. I didn't know what to say. All I knew was how I felt at night. That was what was keeping me awake. The frightening ugly feelings.

"Ana? I'm talking to you… Ana? Are you listening?"

I looked up at Rachel. "What?"

"What's going on? Is something worrying you?"

"No, I'm fine."

"It must be tough, without Ellie. I know how close you two were."

I'd almost forgotten about Ellie. With everything else going on, there hadn't been room to miss her any more. The only person I missed was Mum. Always Mum. And since I'd seen Frances, I was missing her even more.

"I guess I do miss her," I said. Because I didn't know what else to say.

"And Jamie?" she said. "Are things okay with Jamie?"

"What do you mean?"

"Nothing," she said awkwardly. "I'm just asking."

"I'm not seeing Jamie," I said. "If that's what you mean. We're friends. Nothing's happened." I didn't want her to know about me and Jamie. It was all so new.

"That's not what I meant," Rachel said. "But fine, if you're just friends – then fine."

"What? You don't believe me?"

"I believe you, Ana. I just want to find out what's wrong. Something's up. Something's worrying you – I know it is. The way you are at the moment, the crying out in the night..."

"I'm fine. Honestly. You don't need to worry." And as I said it I shifted closer to her and took her hand in mine, to try and prove the point, to try and change the subject, to try and make it better. She couldn't know about any of this. Not ever.

She nodded.

"Maybe we could do something, you and me, after school?" I said. I knew that would make her happy.

"That would be nice," she said, brightening at the suggestion, and she pulled her hand back onto her lap, and patted her knees. "But it'll have to be tomorrow. There's too much going on at work today."

"Okay. Tomorrow," I said and I forced a smile.

"Well, look...if you are sure you're okay then I'd better go into work. I'm late already. But I'll see you this evening." And as she moved forwards, to give me a hug, I closed my eyes. I sat still as she held me. I couldn't hug her back. Because I couldn't bear her not being Mum. Not even for all the lovely things she did for me.

"Oh, Ana," Rachel said, as she drew back and stood up. "I wish just once in a while you'd let me hug you." And even though I wanted to do something, to say something, to make up for it, I just couldn't think of anything that I could do.

When Rachel left I thought about climbing back into bed. I was so tired. But I'd promised I wouldn't bunk off again, and I owed Rachel that much. I grabbed my blue Converse and slung my school shoes in my bag. I'd change at the school gates. I wanted to wear my Converse today. The blue ones were my favourites. I knew they'd make me feel better, for now, and as soon as I pulled them on, they did.

Except as I bent down to put my books in my bag my cheekbone started to ache again where Frances had hit me. I couldn't stop thinking about the blow. Frances's weak hand, her old skin. It hid such strength. Her power frightened me. I should have given her the card back. I knew that. I didn't feel good about the way I'd been or about what I'd done. But she'd hurt me, and I couldn't stop thinking about that, and how it was all that I deserved. Her striking me across the face was actually nothing; nothing compared to what I'd done to her when I'd killed Catherine.

I stood up and pulled my bag onto my back.

I checked my face in the mirror one last time. A pale, unhappy face gazed back, thick make-up covering the bags under my eyes and the bruise on my cheek. I almost didn't recognize myself. I put my hands through my hair to flatten it and then I took a deep breath and opened the front door to leave the house.

"Hi!" said a voice as soon as I stepped out.

Jamie.

He was sat on the front wall in the garden, waiting for me.

"Hi," I said, and as I turned to lock the door I touched my cheek again. I hoped he wouldn't notice the mark.

"I thought we could walk together?" he said.

"Sure," I said. I couldn't quite believe he was here. That he'd been waiting for me.

"You okay?" he said, as we started to walk.

"Yeah. How long have you been waiting?"

"Just a few minutes," he said. "I thought I might have missed you."

I nodded.

"You're wearing your Converse."

"Yeah. My school shoes are in my bag. These blue ones are my old faithfuls," I said, looking down.

"Not feeling blue?" he said.

I shook my head, smiling.

It was a relief to smile.

"I like the blue," he said, and as he said it he slipped his hand in mine and we walked together, quietly, holding hands, almost all the way to school.

And then my phone rang.

"Hello?" It was a woman's voice. Familiar and unfamiliar all at the same time. "Ana?" she said.

"Yes?" I could feel my heart pounding in my ribcage, shaking my frame. I had this feeling like a bomb was about to go off, like it was strapped to me, fused, and ready to blow, but there was nothing I could do.

I let go of Jamie's hand and stopped walking, motioning to him that he should walk on without me. But he didn't.

"Is that Ana?" the voice said again.

"Yes," I said. "Who is this please?"

And as I said it, I knew.

"It's Amanda, Amanda Trees."

I turned away from Jamie and faced the way we'd just walked. I needed the privacy. As I turned it felt like the whole world was turning with me, and I was stood all alone, in the middle of it; the spine of a spinning top, twirling tall, the world fanning out just a little bit faster all around me.

"Amanda," I said. "Yes, it's me." And a single tear left my eye and slipped as smooth as a raindrop on glass down my reddened cheek, the salt burning my skin as it went.

"What is it? Ana?" Jamie whispered, following me around, his face crinkled with concern as he wiped the tear from around my neck.

"I..."

He grabbed my hand, but I shook my head so he would let go and I turned away from him again. My fingers were wrapped around the phone so tightly – I didn't want to drop it...lose her – that I was almost wincing with the grip.

"Is this a bad time?" Mum asked. "I can call back. I wasn't sure—"

"No – it's fine," I said. "I just—"

"Do you need to call me back? This is a bad time, isn't it?"

"I'm on my way to school," I said. "I..." I couldn't form the words to explain.

"No problem," she said. "Maybe later then. Call back when it's good for you. I'm here."

"Okay," I said.

"You'll have my number now, in your phone, won't you?" she said.

"Yes," I said. "Yes, I will."

"Right," she said.

There was a pause.

"Can I ask...how you found me?"

"Frances Wells," she said. "She called. Last night."

I couldn't believe that Frances had done that, after what had happened yesterday.

"So you'll call me?" she said. "We'll speak later?"

"Yes, yes..." I said.

"It is okay, isn't it – that I called?"

"Yes. Yes," I said but somehow I wasn't sure that the sound of my voice convinced her how completely and utterly okay it was that she had called. I never thought that I would see her again. Not really. I'd wished for her. I'd longed for her. But I never truly believed I would ever get to speak to her or see her again. I'd been lost in the surprise and the joy of hearing her voice and I hadn't told her how completely wonderful it was that she had called.

"Right, well, goodbye then..." she said.

"I'm glad," I said quickly, "that you called..."

But there was silence now on the other end of the line, and she had gone.

Jamie was stood a little way up the street, waiting for me.

"Is everything okay?" he said.

"I think so, yeah."

"You looked so sad, just then."

"I'm fine, really," I said.

"Who was it?"

"Someone. No one. Come on. Let's go," I said. "Or we'll be late." And I took his hand in mine again, and I squeezed it, pulling him with me into a run, and as we ran Jamie laughed, and I laughed with him, and I felt so free. *Please*, I thought. *Please let Jamie never have to know about me. Let him never have to know anything bad about me.*

"I'll see you in class," I said when we got to the school gates. "I've got to change these shoes. Go in or you'll be late."

I sat down on the wall by the gates and started to pull at my laces.

"Ana..." Jamie said. "I..." He stopped.

"What?"

We looked at each other.

His eyes held mine.

I willed for him to finish what he was going to say.

I let my eyes scan his gorgeous face while I waited for him to speak.

"I – I guess I'll see you later," he said, taking a step away from me towards the gates.

"Yeah," I said, and I smiled. I wished I knew what he had really wanted to say, but in my heart I thought I knew. Because all I was thinking about was when I was going to kiss him, and I guessed that was what he'd been thinking too.

18.

I went back on the roof today after school.

I couldn't help myself.

Hearing Mum's voice had excited me. The sound of her, the bliss of hearing her again. It made me more Emma than I'd ever felt before, and I liked it. I had twinges in my stomach, nice ones, bright ones, like silver sparklers in the darkness. And each time I replayed the call in my mind, another one was lit. And there was Jamie too – adding to the brightness. This was dangerous – to feel like this – I knew it was. Because I didn't deserve to feel this way.

I pulled myself up onto the roof and laid on my back and looked up at the sky. I didn't let myself blink.

Not even once.

When you lie on your back and look up at the sky without blinking, your eyes fill with sky and your head fills with sky and everything feels...blank.

I lay on the roof with my eyes open and I felt so blank that I wept.

I wept and I wept.

And I wept for myself, not for Catherine, because right now feeling blank – feeling nothing – was far better than feeling all the pain and the guilt that I'd been feeling before.

19.

I came down from the roof because the light was fading and I knew Rachel would be back home any minute.

As soon as I came down all the feelings I'd been feeling since I'd spoken to Mum came rushing back.

I had to tell someone about her. I'd burst into a thousand tiny pieces, disperse, if I couldn't say out loud to someone, "I've spoken to my mum. I've spoken to her!"

I grabbed a drink out of the fridge and stuffed it into my bag.

My heart was beating, fast. I pulled on my coat.

Rachel walked in.

"Ana? Where are you going?"

"Out!" I said. I didn't stop.

"But I've just got in—"

"I won't be long!" I called from the hall, and I went.

I got the bus and I went to The Avenue.

Because Frances was the only person I could talk to about Mum.

I had to go to her.

I had no choice.

I had to.

I banged on the door several times before Frances came to answer.

"It's you," she said, as she opened the door.

"Can I come in?"

"You can, but not for long," she said and she waved her hand to indicate that I should come in, and then she shut the front door behind me. She shut it hard – and as it slammed I had a sudden feeling of regret that I had come.

"Have you had a phone call?" Frances said, as she walked along the hall.

"Yes…" I said, following her through to the sitting room. "I have."

"Sit down," she said.

And I did what she asked. I sat.

I lifted my hair off my face, tucking it behind my ear. I wanted her to see the bruise she'd left when she hit me.

"I called them," Frances said, ignoring me. "Richard and Amanda. I spoke to Amanda and I explained about you."

Her eyes bored into me as she spoke. I felt my eyelids flicker again and again. I didn't know where to look.

What was I doing here? What was I thinking coming here, again?

Suddenly I was so tired.

I shook my head to try and wake myself up.

"Why did you come here today, Ana? To reprimand me for hitting you?" Frances said.

"No!" I said.

"Good," she said.

There was a silence.

"I came because I spoke to her – to Mum. I wanted to tell you, and I wanted to ask you what you said to Amanda about me? When you called?"

"I told her that you'd come to see me, and that you claimed you were Emma. And I passed on your phone number, your address – the details you'd left the last time you were here."

"You said that I *claimed* to be Emma?" I said.

Frances nodded.

"I thought you believed me?"

"Did I say that, Ana? Did I say that I believed you? I'm not sure that I ever did. Anyway, I thought you'd be pleased. I did what you asked me to do: I contacted Amanda and Richard. And now Amanda has contacted you."

"Yes," I said, and I nodded. She was right. She had done what I'd wanted her to do, and Mum had called.

"If I was given the chance to see Catherine again,"

Frances said, "I'd take it now, just as Amanda has done. But I can't. Can I?"

Frances's voice was strong, slow.

"Do you not have anything to say?" Frances said.

"I'm not sure what to say," I said. "Except that I'm sorry I'm not Catherine. I'm sorry I can't bring her back for you, now, when you are old and ill and—"

"Don't you dare pity me, Ana!" Frances interrupted. "I may be old, and I may be ill, but I still have life. And I intend to hold on to it for quite some time yet."

"How can you be so sure of everything?" I said.

"Are you not sure of yourself, Ana? You say that as if you are not sure, but you must have been sure to have come here, to me, like you did. You must have been very sure."

"I've never been so sure," I said. "And so frightened—"

I could feel my hands start to shake.

"Fear can change a person," Frances said. "Make them less strong."

There was a moment between us. Neither of us spoke.

"I'll have tea," Frances said, eventually. "You can make it."

I turned and went straight into the kitchen. I was glad to get out of the room and away from Frances, just for a minute. I found where everything was and made the tea, then gathered the mugs, milk and sugar onto a tray as well as I could and carried it into the front room. Frances started speaking again.

"So will you see them? Amanda and Richard?"

"Yes, I will. If they'll meet me," I said.

"You mustn't be afraid of them," she said.

"Afraid?"

"You'll just have to find a way to persuade them, like you persuaded me."

I looked at Frances. Was she now saying she believed me? That she believed I was Emma? I felt like I was walking on shifting sand; every turn in the conversation with her felt like a test. I never knew whether my next step would be secure, or a slip into softer, deeper ground.

"Everything is so fragile," she said, "isn't it?" And she smiled. My fragility had pleased her, and in one tiny moment between us, as she smiled, I could see that she had once been pretty.

I nodded in reply.

Fragile. I knew exactly what she meant. Except if you'd asked me to explain it, I wouldn't have known how.

"Catherine loved you. She idolized you. 'Emma Trees,' she would say. 'This was Emma Trees's jumper…' 'Emma Trees had this book…' 'I want a room at the top of the house like Emma Trees…' Do you remember that?"

I shook my head.

"No," she said. "I guess you wouldn't. Catherine was

waiting to see you when you came over that evening. Do you remember how excited she was the night of the party?"

"No," I said.

Because suddenly I was filled with another memory. I could see Dad carrying a baking tray into a kitchen. There were other people in the room, moving about, getting things out of the oven. I was carrying a tray too. Mine was full of cheese twists. They looked dry. Some of the cheese had turned black on the baking tray, sticking to the metal like burned rocks. Dad sat his tray on the side and then leaned over and took mine from me, to set it down next to his. And then he turned and put his hand on Mum's shoulder. He told her that he was going to take me over for a play on the Green. He said that we would knock for Frances and Catherine and come back over with them for half past six. And I remembered Mum's face when he'd said that. She'd smiled. But I could see it was a smile that you put on for other people; for the woman who was stood next to her, and for him, for Dad, and for me. Mainly I think she smiled for me.

The memory of it hurt.

"You remember Richard bringing you here though?" Frances said.

"Yes," I said. "I do."

We had left the Williamses' and walked out onto The Avenue and I remembered running alongside him to try and keep up. He was walking fast. I'd held on to his big warm hand and I'd pulled at him to try and make him come with me onto the Green. I'd pulled on him until my feet left the ground and I was swinging against his legs. I wanted him to play with me on the Green – like he'd said – like he'd promised. But he was knocking at Frances's door now. I wasn't going to give up trying to get his attention. Frances answered the door. And even though I knew that however much I pulled on his arms, I'd never be able to move him, I kept hanging off him as he stood in the hall, talking, so he couldn't ignore me. Eventually he shook me off, like rain from an umbrella, and I stumbled a little. I was never going to win this battle, and it hurt.

It still hurt now.

I sighed. I could feel a sob crouching low in my chest. I heaved with it as I took a breath in. I stood up and walked over to the bookshelves in the alcoves next to the fireplace. Frances was watching me all the time. I could feel her look, her stare.

"You were wearing a navy dress and boots. You looked nice," I said, eventually. I could see her, in my mind. Her hair around her neck. Soft, gentle.

I touched the books. Here were the same books that had sat on these same shelves the night Catherine had died. The night that I was here when I was Emma. The thought that they were still here, unmoved, unchanged, but I was here, now, in another life – it frightened me.

"I wore it for the party," she said. "But of course, I never made it there in the end."

"Dad said he'd come in a minute, that he'd come out with me and Catherine in a minute. That he would play with us. He told us to go out and play with the ball." I ran my fingers across the spines of the books as I spoke, and I felt cold as I touched them.

"We've gone over this already," Frances said. "Too many times."

I shivered.

"No, we haven't!" I said.

"You sound like Emma when you say that," Frances said. "You are so like her when you say that."

I moved my shoulders to release the shivers in my back. I was cold. Even the insides of my bones felt like they'd caught the chill.

"We're going to the river, Catherine. We'll play hide-and-seek by the river."

"If you don't play I'll tell on you. You have to come or that's what I'll do."

I turned to look at Frances.

I didn't speak.

"We watched you and Catherine go over the road and onto the Green," she said. "We didn't leave you to cross on your own."

"Dad blew me a kiss. And Catherine. He blew us both a kiss, from the window. He was standing in the window and he blew us both a kiss."

"Yes," Frances said.

"And you closed the curtains. I saw you. You closed them."

Frances nodded.

"Why?"

She'd shut me out.

"You were with Dad..." I said.

She was with Dad, and she'd shut me and Catherine out.

I was in territory I didn't know enough about. I was so cold I started to shake. Frances was staring at me, all the time. I tried hard to keep myself still, but I couldn't keep hold of my body. I didn't want to think the thought that I was thinking—

"You were with Dad," I said. "What were you...?"

"I was in love – with Richard – with your father," she said.

I felt my throat close up.

I didn't want to cry.

"He didn't come and play – because of you?" I said.

I started to cry.

"You closed the curtains and you left us..." I said.

"That's right," Frances said.

"You left me – with Catherine – without my dad..."

"You were always a daddy's girl, always jealous. You wanted to be with him all the time," Frances said, almost scowling now.

And I saw them – as I saw them then – when I had peeked through the letter box that night – Frances's legs bare and the skirt of her dress way up high as she lay back on the stairs – Dad kissing her, kissing her arms, her neck – and I didn't want to keep looking, but I did – and I heard Dad say Frances's name like a whisper between the kisses – and I wanted to cry and scream with the hate – so much hate – and I didn't understand – I didn't understand – and I didn't want him to be doing this...

"*No!*" I'd screamed.

And I saw Frances's head turn, just slightly, towards the front door, and I pulled away from the letter box and it banged shut.

I faced the Green, panicking now. I'd left Catherine at the river. I hadn't told anyone where I'd left her or how I'd left her. And now I'd seen this – my dad – and Frances – and I had to hide. It was bad. It was all so bad. And I ran and hid behind the bins in the front garden, next to the wall with the rough-cut petals, because I had to hide. Because no one could know what I'd seen and what I'd done—

"You aren't listening to me, Ana." Frances's voice momentarily broke through.

I'd taken Catherine to the river and I'd told her to go and hide, and then I'd followed her. She'd thought I was counting, and I was, but I was looking through the gaps between my fingers and I was watching her go. I saw where she hid. I waited for her to go quiet. Completely quiet. I made sure she wasn't going to come back to me, or to the house again. I did that. And then I left her. I knew it wasn't right, but I didn't want to play with her. I left her at the river and went and knocked on Frances's door for my dad. But still, he didn't come. I'd stood and I'd waited and I'd looked through the letter box… It was all so bad – I had to hide – I had to hide from them all. Me and Catherine, we were meant to be playing hide-and-seek. It was getting dark. It was my turn to hide now. I'd hide in the dark so no one could find me. I didn't want anyone to find me. Not now. Not ever. It had to be my turn to hide – and then no one could ever ask me what I did—

"Ana?" Frances said.

I turned and I stared back at her, hard.

"You never came for us," I said. "For me or for Catherine. No one came."

tuesday

20.

Rachel brought me a cup of tea in bed the next morning.

I woke slowly. The first thing I thought of was Mum. I hadn't called her. I'd said I'd call her back, and I hadn't. I wanted to call her. I needed to. But after I'd seen Frances, after remembering what I'd seen, I didn't feel like I could call. Not just yet. I didn't know what I would say to her about me, about her, about any of it.

"It's almost seven. I left you as long as I could, but I need to go in early today."

"Okay," I said, turning in the bed to face her, slowly opening my eyes.

"Did you sleep better last night?" she asked, sitting on the edge of the bed.

I'd been awake most of the night thinking about Frances, thinking about Dad, and most of all thinking about Mum and whether she had known what was going on.

"Kind of," I said.

"So are we still going to do something this afternoon?"

I'd actually completely forgotten that I'd suggested it, but I pretended I hadn't. I nodded.

"I was thinking it'd be nice to go into Richmond," she said. "We can have a burger in that diner you like."

"Sure," I said, stretching my legs so that they stuck out from under the duvet.

"Great. I'll put some toast on for you before I go." And she stood up and went downstairs.

We met after school and walked over the bridge into Richmond. It was a gorgeous day, and as we walked together I stopped to take it all in. There was a heron stood high on a willow, and boats, gently rocking, in the water by the boat sheds. It was so peaceful. Rachel came and stood next to me.

"David always loved it here," she said.

I looked at her. "David – my dad?" I couldn't believe she'd mentioned David. She never normally did.

"Yes. I always think of him when I walk over this bridge," she said.

"You've never told me that before."

"Haven't I?"

"So what happened? With you and David, I mean?"

"I've told you before," she started to say. "I'm sure—"

"That was ages ago."

"We were together, I got pregnant, he couldn't handle it and he left," Rachel said.

"How long were you together, before I came along?"

"Four years," she said.

"Did you love him?"

"Yes, I did," she said, more quietly now. "We loved each other very much."

She'd never said that before. It was reassuring, to hear her say it, to know that they had loved each other once, in the beginning. That was something at least.

"What was he like?" I asked.

"God, now there's a question! I'm not sure I can remember," she said.

I hated it when she did that. Dismissed stuff. But then I wondered whether maybe you wouldn't remember what someone was like fifteen years ago. Maybe the way Rachel remembered David wasn't that different to the way I remembered being Emma. Perhaps when it comes down to it, we all only know each other as much as this.

"Would you try and remember?" I said, and Rachel looked at me. I could tell she didn't really want to remember but knew she was going to try. For me.

"Okay... Well...he was grumpy in the mornings. And he was funny. We did laugh, a lot. I remember that."

"Except in the mornings..." I said.

"Yes!" she said, smiling. "Except in the mornings." She

paused. "He was generous. He'd always be the first to buy a round in the pub, even if he was broke. Which he often was."

"What did he do?"

"He was a sound engineer. Spent all day in a music studio. No light. I think that brought him down a bit."

"What, he didn't like it?"

"No, he liked it. I'm just not sure it was that good for him. He'd get low. Sad. Kind of depressed. But, what do I know? He left me for the twenty-one-year-old receptionist in the end," she said and all the softness went out of her voice.

I'd always known he'd found someone else, that he'd left Rachel seven months pregnant with me, but still, when she said it like that it struck a blow. For me. For Rachel. That was our loss.

Rachel put her arm through mine. "But do you know how happy I was when you were born?" she said. I remembered, this was always her way to repair the damage of this story.

I smiled and shook my head. I liked to hear her say it, despite everything.

"I was the happiest woman alive in the world ever, ever, ever!" she said, and she squeezed me. And for a moment I almost felt like I could have hugged her – really hugged her – but I didn't. I squeezed her arm back, quickly, gently and I smiled. And I hoped that, for her, it was enough.

My phone rang.

It was Jamie.

Rachel scooped her arm out from within mine. "You take that," she said and walked on a couple of steps ahead.

"Hi," I said.

"Hi."

I thought about the last time I'd seen him – and how it had been.

"I just wanted to see how you are. What you're doing?" he said.

"I'm out. With Rachel. We're in Richmond."

"Nice," he said. "Or is it?"

"It's okay," I said, smiling. "What're you up to?"

"Not much," he said. "Just thinking about when I'm going to see you...just you."

My stomach rolled, and like a curling wave along an endless shore, it just kept rolling.

"Well, how about tomorrow?" I said, smiling. "After school?"

"Yeah," he said. "Great."

And he rung off, and as I put the phone in my pocket I felt a rushing, a glowing.

"That was Jamie," I said, catching Rachel up.

"I guessed," she said.

"I'm going to meet him, tomorrow, after school."

"All right. But I don't want you back late. Not like last night."

"Okay," I said. Rachel hadn't said anything about me running out when she got in last night, and I was doing my best to avoid having to talk about it.

"I know I've said this before, but I want you to know you can always talk to me, if you need to. You do know that, don't you?"

"Yes," I said, and I started to walk on.

"I worry that there's stuff going on with you that you're not telling me. I can't help if you don't tell me."

"I'm fine, Rachel," I said. "Honestly. Let's not talk about this now."

"Well, I would have talked to you about it last night, but you ran out."

I didn't answer.

"I don't know where you went, and today, you look so tired." She paused and looked at me, waiting for an answer.

I didn't say anything.

"You're still not sleeping, are you?"

"It's okay," I said. I didn't want her to fuss over me. I hadn't slept for a week now, but still I didn't want her to make a fuss.

We carried on walking.

"Grillie tells me you go and see Frances Wells, at her home. Is that right?" Rachel said.

"How does Grillie know that?" I said, pulling my arm out from hers, stopping and turning to face her.

"Because she and Frances speak. They've seen each other a couple of times since they were in hospital together. They play bridge."

"I didn't know that!" I said.

The thought that Frances might talk to Grillie – that she might tell Grillie about me – it terrified me.

"I should have known that. Somebody should have told me!" I said.

"What do you mean somebody should have told you?"

I wanted to run away. I couldn't run away. I knew that. I had to stay and speak to Rachel, or it would all look too weird.

Rachel went on. "Grillie said you didn't go over and see her last week—"

"So?" I interrupted.

"She's upset, Ana! She likes seeing you. She's just out of hospital for God's sake!"

I took a step back, away from Rachel, to try and break the conversation. To try and get some space, in my head. I was frightened.

"Ana, what's going on? This mood, this change in you, it's not like you at all."

"Well, so what if I go and visit Frances? What does it

matter to you or to Grillie? It's none of your business what I do!"

"I think it's lovely that you go. Honestly. I do. I'm just trying to work out what's changed—"

"What do you mean?"

"Well, with you not sleeping, and walking out of school – and it's all so unlike you, Ana, and it's all happened in the past week or so. Or was it something at the party? Did something happen at the party?"

"I told you, nothing happened at the party!"

"So what is it? Something's wrong. I know it is. I know you, Ana."

I looked at her and I felt my eyes fill up with tears.

She didn't know me.

She didn't know me at all.

"If it's something I've done," she said, "I mean, I know it's not the best situation – me not being with David…"

I took in a deep breath to steady myself. I hated seeing her upset like this. I missed Mum. I wanted my dad. Not David. But I couldn't tell her that. I couldn't say it. I couldn't explain.

And suddenly I felt trapped. I just wanted to get away because she couldn't know what I was thinking or what I was feeling. She couldn't know about any of it.

My pulse started throbbing, my mind wrestling with itself, trying to find the right words, to make it better.

I had to leave, to get on the roof, to the space on the roof.

I looked up.

Rachel was crying now.

She was stood in the street crying, and people were looking at us.

"You're a great mum...really, you are," I said.

And I meant it, because she was.

"Do you think you might ever call me 'Mum'?" Rachel said, looking up at me now.

"No—" I said it quickly, without thinking. Too quickly. "I don't know..."

Rachel got a tissue out of her bag and wiped her face with it.

We stood, still, together, for a moment.

"Shall we go? Get something to eat now?" I said.

"Yes," she said. "Are you hungry?"

And even though I didn't feel like I could eat a thing, I said yes, and I went and I ate. For her. For Rachel.

21.

When we got home I went straight up to my room and put my music on loud. Rachel was on the phone to Grillie. I didn't want to hear their conversation. Now that I knew Grillie and Frances were in regular contact, it made me feel on edge when Grillie called. I just wanted to get away. To be on my own.

I kicked off my shoes and I opened the window wide. And as I manoeuvred my way from the bedroom and up onto the roof I let go of the bathroom window ledge with one of my hands.

It was just for a few seconds.

But I let go.

It was an accident.

My hand just slipped.

But for those few long seconds, as I hung with my one hand gripped tight to the ledge and my other reaching to join it, I felt free.

Because I didn't feel anything.

No guilt. No pain.

Only the space around me, and it was white and clean and bright.

Blank…

Just for a moment…

I was blank…

And in my mind, it was calm.

22.

When I came down from the roof, I had a bath and got into bed, but I couldn't sleep. I went down to get some water. Rachel was watching TV. I sat down next to her on the sofa, but I didn't watch, because I was thinking about meeting Jamie tomorrow and how his call today had made me feel.

I knew I wanted to kiss him.

And I imagined over and over how it might be while the images on the TV shone brightly on the screen.

My phone rang.

UNKNOWN NUMBER.

"Take it in the other room, will you?" Rachel said.

I stood up and walked through to the kitchen, rubbing my eyes as I went.

"Hello?"

"Ana?"

"Yes."

"It's Frances."

I didn't reply. I didn't want to speak to her. Not yet anyway. I was still trying to get the images of her and Dad out of my head.

"Are you still there, Ana?" she said.

"What is it?" I said, whispering so Rachel couldn't hear.

"You haven't come to see me."

"I came yesterday," I said.

"I've been waiting," she said. "Today. Did you call Amanda back?"

"No – not yet. I—"

"But you will?" she said.

"Yes," I said.

There was silence.

"I want to see you again, Ana," she said. "Once you've spoken to her. Will you come?"

"Yes," I said. I just wanted to get her off the phone. I didn't want to talk to her and I didn't want Rachel to hear me having this conversation.

"Good," she said. "Because obviously, I will want to know what she says to you. There are to be no secrets between us now, Ana."

"Secrets?" I said, peering through to check that Rachel was still watching TV. "How can you say that when you must have lived a life full of them!"

I was thinking about Dad and Frances again. I didn't

want to think about them. I couldn't bear to think about them, together.

"And I know you see my grandma," I carried on. "You say there should be no secrets but you never told me that you see Grillie!"

"Your grandma came over on Sunday afternoon after you left. We played bridge," she said.

"Why didn't you tell me?" I said, my voice getting louder.

"I've always played bridge, Ana."

I waited a moment before I spoke. "You haven't told Grillie about me, have you? About Emma?" I said. My voice sounded weak. I felt weak. "Please, Frances," I said. "*Please* tell me you haven't told her."

"What would I say, Ana?"

I thought I might cry, but I held on to the tears because I could hear Rachel moving about next door.

"It was hard enough telling Amanda about you," Frances carried on. "So – no. I haven't told anyone else."

"Thank you," I whispered.

"You sound tired, Ana. Are you tired?"

"Yes," I said.

Suddenly I was so tired. I felt utterly deadbeat.

"It can make life quite bewildering – when you don't sleep – don't you find?"

I opened my mouth to speak.

"It's hard to know what's real and what's not."

She was right. I was so tired. And I didn't have the fight I needed for this conversation any more.

"You should try and get some sleep," Frances said.

"Yes," I said.

"You'll visit, when you've spoken to Amanda," she said.

"I will," I said.

And then she hung up.

And I went and lay down on my bed and slept for six hours straight.

I did exactly as Frances told me to.

wednesday

23.

When I woke early the next morning all I could feel was the loss of Mum. It was a feeling I'd lived with my whole life. It was normal. The norm. It was all I knew. Except since I'd seen Frances it had got worse. So much worse. It was like an ache deep inside that I couldn't soothe. And here I was, with her number in my phone. I could call her, I could speak to her, and yet somehow it unnerved me.

All I had to do was press CALL.

I closed my eyes and told myself to do it.

And I did.

Mum answered immediately.

"It's Ana," I said. "We spoke – before – earlier in the week..."

"Ana!" she said. She sounded pleased. "I didn't think you were going to call back."

Her voice was just as I remembered it, although – like the crackles on a glaze – it showed its age now. I'd forgotten that she wouldn't be exactly as I remembered her. I'd forgotten she'd be older now. Not that it mattered, because here I was – speaking to her. And I was so relieved. My whole body relaxed at the sound of her. If a person could shine, I'm sure, in that moment, I would have been shining.

"It's not too early, is it?" I said. "I just wasn't sure when else I could call."

"It's fine," she said.

"I'm sorry, I know I said I'd call straight back, but—"

"Don't be sorry," she said.

Neither of us spoke.

"I – I wonder…could we meet?" I said. "It seems a bit hard, to talk like this, on the phone."

"Okay," she said. "Let me get my diary."

The phone clunked as she put it down, and I heard her walk across a hard floor. There she was. My mum. My real mum. I was going to see her again.

We arranged to meet the following day. A cafe in Hampton Wick. She said it wasn't that far from Twickenham, where I lived. She said it was a nice cafe, although she hadn't been for a while, but she was sure it was still there. She said she could get there by ten. I listened to her and I smiled to hear her talk. The familiarity of her was overwhelming. I didn't care about the cafe. I didn't even question that I'd have to skip school again. I just wanted to see her. Tomorrow wasn't going to be soon enough.

"I'll have to bring the dog," she said. "Do you like dogs?"

"Yes, yes, I do."

"Oh, good. He's a black Lab," she said. "He has a red collar. He's chunky. If you look out for him, you'll be sure to find me. I'll be on the other end of the lead!" she said and she laughed.

"But I'm pretty sure I'll recognize you – without the dog – I mean…"

She stopped laughing. "Right," she said, and then she paused. "Really?"

"Well, yes," I said. "Of course."

"Well – okay," she said. "I'll see you tomorrow, then." And I could hear the change in her voice as she said it, like she was unsure, frightened even, and I wished I hadn't said a thing.

24.

I felt sick all day at school.

I wasn't sure whether it was the thought of seeing Jamie at the end of the day that was making me feel this way or whether it was because I was seeing Mum tomorrow. Either way I felt sick; it was a heady mix of excitement and fear and hope that was making me feel this way, and it was new. It was all new.

"Hey," Jamie said as the bell went and everyone started to move towards the door.

"Hey," I said back.

"Where shall we go?"

I shrugged. I actually hadn't thought about it.

"I was thinking the park. We can pick up something to eat or drink on the way," he said. "If you want to?"

I nodded and smiled, and Jamie took my hand and we started to walk.

We found a bench by the ponds. We'd bought coffees

at the kiosk but I still felt so sick I wasn't sure I could drink mine. And it was hot. Too hot. I set the cup down next to me at my feet and I felt Jamie move in closer as I bent down. I tucked my legs beneath me and sat back up.

There was no conversation we could have right now.

The air we were breathing, the thoughts we were thinking were permeated only with the possibility of our kiss, and I could feel only the anticipation of it between us.

"Listen, Ana – I..."

I turned to face him on the bench.

"Can I—?"

And I didn't wait for him to say it. I didn't wait for him to ask whether he could kiss me. I just let my eyes search his beautiful face, and I looked at his lips and I lifted my hands up to hold him, to touch his cheeks, and as he came closer towards me I pulled him in and our lips met, and our mouths gently opened to each other – and we kissed – we were kissing...

...and it was blissful.

It was the most blissful thing that had ever happened to me in my whole entire life.

And I held on to the moment

– and I held on to him

– and it was perfect.

thursday

25.

I didn't sleep. Sleeplessness was a permanent part of my life now. This morning my head ached with it. But at least when I told Rachel that I had a headache, and that I needed to stay off school, to sleep, it wasn't that much of a lie. I said I'd go in later, and she was okay with that.

I waited for her to leave the house, then pulled on my jeans and a sweatshirt, grabbed my bag and coat and headed straight to the station. I didn't want to risk being late.

When I got to the station I could see that the next train to Hampton Wick was at 8.52 a.m. I was going to be massively early. I sat on the platform and texted Jamie while I waited.

Not in this morning but will be later. Headache. Need to sleep. Thinking of you. Ax

I felt sick again when I sent it. It was true, I was

thinking of him, but as I hit SEND I felt like somehow I'd said too much.

I bought a hot chocolate. It tasted nothing like hot chocolate. I opened up the lid and looked inside. It looked like it was just brown sugary water. I didn't mind. I needed the sweetness, to keep me going. The granules crunched in my teeth, and I liked it. I put on my headphones and listened to my music and the train pulled in on time.

I stepped on and sat, gazing out of the window. I thought again about what Frances had said to Mum. She'd said that I was someone who claimed to be Emma. It didn't sound very convincing. More like total madness. And yet Mum was coming to meet me, now. Frances must have said something more. She must have. Why else would Mum be coming? To Mum, I was a stranger. A fifteen-year-old stranger. To me, she was Mum, and I had to find a way to persuade her to accept me and to love me, like she had loved me before, like I had loved her, like I still loved her now. Because I was so sure that if I could see her again, if we were together again, I'd feel better. I'd feel like me. All of me.

I got off at Hampton Wick and walked from the station towards the shops. I searched the faces of everyone I walked past, urgently seeking Mum out. Her face was there, in my mind, all the time. Her soft blonde hair resting against her pale cheek. And yet the more I looked for her in the street, the less I felt I could see. As I turned the corner I saw the cafe where we were supposed to meet. There was an old man sat outside with a newspaper and a coffee, and a woman smoking in an apron, leaning against the door frame. There was no one else around.

I looked back up the street and started scanning my view for dogs. There was a small yappy thing tied up outside a newsagent's. I wished it would be quiet. It wouldn't stop barking for its owner to come out of the shop.

I was getting closer to the cafe now, and still, I couldn't see her. For a split second I doubted myself – what if I didn't recognize her? What if I'd walked past her already? What if I had to go home without seeing her because I never found her? Because this woman I think I know isn't here? What then?

As I walked I felt hopeless, like someone had turned my heart inside out and emptied its contents onto the side of the road.

I stopped walking, and stood utterly still.

I felt in that moment as if I had nothing, and no one.

And then I saw her.

Mum.

There she was. Walking along the street, towards the cafe, like today was the most ordinary day, like she was the most ordinary woman alive. Except to me – she was everything, and today was no ordinary day. It was just she didn't know it yet.

I ran across the road. I didn't even look as I stepped out. I just wanted to get to her. She must have left the dog at home, because there was no dog, no black Lab, no red collar. She looked old. She was old. Of course she was. Her hair was grey now, not blonde, her walk slower, her back a little more curved than I remembered it. I hesitated for a moment as I neared her. I slowed myself down. It was her. I knew it was her. I *knew* her. I stepped up onto the pavement. She stood outside the cafe, her back to me now. I walked up to her and I touched her on the arm. She turned around to face me.

"Hi," I said, and when she saw me she smiled, and I thought I might scream out with the joy of it.

I loved her.

And she was here.

"You must be Ana!" she said. "Well, it's very nice to meet you."

I nodded and I swept my hand across my face to wipe away the tears. I was crying with relief and happiness and with sadness – to see her – but to see her so old, like this. It wasn't what I had imagined or expected.

"I left the dog at home in the end," she said. "Let's go inside." And she opened the cafe door to let me go in first and as she did she looked at me, searching my face for something, for some recognition. I prayed that there would be something in my face that was Emma.

We sat at a corner table and ordered tea. I wondered whether the dog, or the lack of it, had been some kind of test.

She stirred her tea, and then she spoke. "Emma never used to drink tea," she said. "She didn't like the taste."

"Oh…right. I do," I said. "Well, I didn't as a kid, but I do now…"

If the dog was a test, I'd passed. If the tea was a test, I'd fallen short at the start.

She sipped from her mug and her eyes darted about the room. I could tell the tea was too hot and that she'd stung her lip but was holding in the pain. She was more nervous than I was.

"I'm not really sure what we say," she said. "In a situation like this."

"I know," I said, looking at her hands, at her rings. She wore the same rings she always wore, but her fingers were wider around the knuckles and her skin was lined and brown in places with age. These were the hands I remembered, and yet not the hands I'd held and stroked and pulled on as a child.

We were quiet again.

"I don't know what Frances said to you," I said. "About me."

Mum frowned and I could see all the lines on her face – the lines marking the years I'd missed with her.

I saw myself in our kitchen. I was smaller. I could hear shouting above me, and I could see all the breadcrumbs nestling under the toaster from where I stood. I tried to block the shouting out. I felt tiny, insignificant, like a mouse in a storm. Mum and Dad were shouting. Mum's arms were waving about and the wide sleeves of her dressing gown were flapping like some kind of prehistoric bird's wings. Dad was pacing, threatening at every step to just walk out of the room, but Mum reeled him back in again with more words, angry ones. I'd only wanted cornflakes. I just wanted the cornflakes. Would someone not just get me the cornflakes? "STOP SHOUTING!" I'd said, "STOP SHOUTING!" And they did.

"Frances didn't say very much," Mum said.

I nodded.

"And D—" I went to say "Dad" but I stopped myself. "Richard," I said. "Is he…?"

"What?" she said.

"Does he know? I mean…that Frances called?"

I could feel myself getting tied up in knots. I didn't know what Mum knew about Dad and Frances. I didn't want to say anything, to give anything away, but I needed to know whether he knew about me, now.

"Yes," she said. "He knows, but I'm afraid he's not –

well, he's not convinced – if that's the word. Or at least he doesn't think he could ever be convinced. He's not interested in meeting you. Not right now, anyway."

I nodded.

He didn't want to see me.

That felt like a blow. A blow that hit me deep in my belly.

I wanted my dad. It wasn't the same feeling as wanting Mum, but it was there. I needed him. Like I needed him that night, with Catherine.

"So what do you know – about Emma?" Mum said. "I'd like to know."

"I remember the curtains in my bedroom. They were white with green flowers. And the walls, they had matching wallpaper, the same pattern, but green on white. I remember tracing the gaps between the flowers with my fingers when I lay awake at night."

"Go on," she said.

"I remember that Dad let me collect up the grass into a bucket after he'd mowed the lawn. I remember you used to talk to the car. You used to ask it to start, when it was cold and it wouldn't go. You'd say, 'Please, please start. We love you, car,' and when it didn't start we'd sit for a minute or two before trying again. When it eventually started, we'd cheer! I remember a shop, full of clothes. I don't know where that was. I remember a hall…I didn't like it there.

It had one yellow wall with framed pictures all over it, set really close together. Maybe someone's house…?"

Mum nodded like she knew the place, but I could see she was holding so much emotion in her throat that she couldn't speak.

"I remember loads more, but mostly, I remember you…" I said. "Just being with you…"

She blew her nose on a pale blue hanky with a pink rose embroidered in the corner of it. I thought about how I'd played with all her scarves and handkerchiefs – ones just like this – when I was little and I used to go through her drawers.

"Why do you think you remember these things?" she said. Her eyes were fixed on me now.

"I don't know. Being Emma – it's just always been there. It's what I've always known. But recently, I've had new memories. It's been more painful, more difficult."

"Difficult?" she said.

"Catherine."

"What about Catherine?" she said, lowering her eyes. She looked different, suddenly. Angry even, like someone who'd been provoked.

"Catherine's death," I said, "and what happened…"

"What happened that night, the consequences of that night, it was all…"

"What?"

"Heartbreaking," she said.

"For Frances," I said, nodding.

"Yes, of course. For Frances. For all of us."

"I wish—"

"There's no use in wishing now," Mum said, her voice dry and taut, like it might crack and split with the pain. "I used to tell you that – then. All the time. Wishing will change nothing." And although her face was full of blackness, for a few seconds, it didn't matter. It didn't matter at all, because I knew then, when she spoke to me, that she believed me. She was talking to me as Emma. She knew I was her Emma.

I searched her face for what to say next. I was desperate to say so much but I didn't know where to start. I opened my mouth to speak, but before I could say anything she had stood up and walked out of the cafe.

I followed her out.

She was waiting for me.

"I'm sorry," she said. "I needed some air."

I put my arms around her. It was all I could think to do. I pressed myself against her chest and held on to her like I would never let her go, and I smelled her smell and the warmth of her, and I found our imprint – the one that had always been there, since I was bundled and born – the one that made us fit.

After a moment or two I could feel her body start

to shake. She was weak, weaker than she was before. Her chest rose and fell as she took a breath, and then she closed herself back into me, her arms wrapped around my shoulders and we stood, enveloped in each other – strangers – family – apart – yet connected.

"There's so much to say, but I'm not sure I can say it," she said and she held on to both my hands with hers.

"I need to know how she died," I said. "Catherine. I just need to know."

Mum dropped my hands. "I don't want to talk about that. That was the worst night of all our lives. It was the beginning of the end of everything good. Surely you must know that? If you are Emma you would know that better than anyone."

She took a step back from me.

"Tell me," I whispered. "Please."

"This is too much," she said, "for one day." And she motioned with her hands that she was going to leave, to say goodbye, and I could see she was about to break down.

"Please – don't go," I said. "I didn't mean to—"

"No!" she said. "I can't do this. I've only just met you. I don't know anything about you."

"Yes, you do! Don't you see?"

"See what?"

"That I'm here, that I'm Emma, that I'm feeling the things that Emma felt, that I have these memories – her memories – that I need to know about that night, about Catherine."

"What I see," she said, "is a young, vibrant girl, Ana. In the here and now. Yes, I hear you speak of things only Emma can know, and I'll admit that's strange – extraordinary – almost wonderful. But…Catherine. I just can't… I'm sorry."

"But if I hadn't seen Frances—"

"Ah, Frances!" she said. "Frances put you up to this. I should have known… As if we all haven't suffered enough."

"No! No one put me up to this. I saw Frances. In the hospital. By chance. It was by chance – and I asked her – for your address – I wanted to see you!"

"I have known Frances for a very long time," Mum said. "And if there is one thing I am certain of, it is that she will never let what happened that night be laid to rest. Never."

"And what about Dad?" I said. "Has he laid it to rest?"

I hadn't meant to say it – Dad.

It just came out.

Mum flinched, when I said it.

"We have too many unanswered questions of our own," she said. "Can't you see that?"

"I thought you'd understand," I said, so softly now.

She took a step towards me. "I can see something of Emma in you," she said. "I can." And she reached out and stroked some hair across my forehead where it had fallen in front of my eyes. "I don't know what it is, but it's there."

"I love you…" I said.

"I loved you," she said back. "So much, my Emma."

A car beeped its horn, and she looked over her shoulder.

"I've got to go," she said, and she walked towards a large silver car that was pulling up alongside us. As she opened the door, she spoke. "I'll be in touch. I'll definitely be in touch. Goodbye, Ana," she said.

I watched her get into the car, and I didn't take my eyes off her for a second. I saw her turn and say something to the driver as she put on her seat belt. I crouched down lower. The driver was wearing a pale brown coat. I could see his hands on the steering wheel, set in place, sturdy, strong, ready to go. And then he glanced over, at Mum, and so, too, at me.

It was my dad.

And he didn't even want to say hello.

friday

26.

I had a nightmare.

About me – facing a polar bear. It's white in the dream. Everywhere is white. The bear is white and I'm in a white world. It's hard to see. It's bright and the light burns my eyes. But I can see the bear. Wherever I am, I can see it. And it terrifies me that I can see it. It terrifies me that I know it will attack. It terrifies me that there is only white space all around me, and nowhere to go, nowhere to hide, no one to help me in this white wilderness.

I think to myself, in the dream, *This is my worst nightmare – to be here – with a bear*. And in the dream I'm saying out loud to myself, "This is my worst nightmare – to be here – with a bear!"

And the polar bear is padding his way towards me, low and heavy. His swagger is strong. And even in the brightness I can see he is coming for me, and then – just as if someone has flicked a switch in my head – I decide not to be afraid. I decide to face it; to face the bear. I think to myself, *I'll face it and see what happens. The worst that can happen is that I'll wake up.*

And so I go towards the bear and the bear comes towards me and it stands on its two back legs and opens its wide mouth. I can see deep inside its red throat, and I can see all of its brown teeth.

It is preparing to kill me.

It is going to savage me.

I know this.

And I go up close to it, really close, and I lift my arm to its face, and I place my hand in its open mouth, and I turn my head away and I wait for the pain.

And I feel nothing.

No pain. No fear. Nothing.

And I look at the bear, and the bear looks at me, and I bring my arm back to my side, and the bear lowers himself down onto all fours and then he sits.

I sit down too.

I mirror him.

And we sit like this for I don't know how long. And we look at each other. And now me and the bear are friends. True friends. I know this as much as I know everything else that I know.

And I am calm.

And now I wonder.

I wonder whether this is what it will feel like when I come to die.

27.

"Are you okay in there?" Rachel's voice was on the other side of the door. I looked at the clock. It was 2.34 a.m.

"Yeah," I said.

Rachel didn't respond. I heard a creak on the landing, and I waited to see what she would do. I heard her go downstairs. A light went on; the kettle began to rumble. I looked at my clock again. It was 2.41 a.m.

I lay there for about half an hour, and whatever I did, however I shifted, I just couldn't go back to sleep. The images of my dream were still vivid in my mind and they were there, with me, every time I closed my eyes; the brightness, the feeling of terror as the bear raised itself up. When I thought about it I felt dread and fear, right at the core of me.

I'd died before. When I was Emma. I would have to die again.

3.12 a.m. Rachel was still downstairs. I couldn't stay alone in bed any longer, so I went down.

"Hi," she said. "Do you want some warm milk?"

We used to have warm milk like this if I woke in the night, when I was little.

"With sugar?"

"Yep, with sugar," she said, smiling.

I sat down in the warmth of her seat while she got up and prepared the milk. It felt nice. Safe. She had always been a good mum. A really good mum.

"Bad dream again?" she said.

I nodded.

"How's the headache?"

"Better," I said.

"Good."

Rachel was moving around the kitchen now, opening and closing the fridge, taking the mugs off the shelf. "I couldn't sleep either," she said. "Too much in my head."

"Do you think about David much?" I said, after a moment.

"Not really. Why?"

"Because you talked about him, the other day. You haven't mentioned him in ages. I was thinking…"

"Is that what's keeping you awake at night?" she said, turning to look at me for a moment.

I shook my head.

"Do you think he'd ever come and find me, though? Do you think he'd ever want to meet me?"

There was a pause.

"Hard to say," she said.

"Are you still in touch with him?"

"No," she said quickly, and when she did she looked at me, a glance, and I saw it. Guilt. I'd recognize it anywhere.

"Did he ever come and see me?" I asked. "When I was born?"

"What's that?" she said as she poured the milk into the cup and stirred in the sugar. I knew she'd heard me. She was playing for time.

"I haven't ever met him – have I?" I asked again.

"He came once. When you were tiny. You wouldn't remember."

"When?"

"I don't know. You must have been six or seven weeks old. Does it matter? You were too young to remember."

"And what happened?"

"Well, he came. He saw you. He brought you Brownie, and he left."

"Brownie came from him?" Brownie was my soft dog, my comfort, the thing that had come everywhere with me when I was a toddler.

"Yes," she said, still stirring, her back towards me.

"Rachel!" I said. "You never told me…!" I was angry, but I didn't know what to do with the anger, so I laughed as I said it. I couldn't believe she hadn't told me.

"What does it matter where Brownie came from?" Rachel said, passing me the warm mug.

"Didn't you think I'd want to know? David is my dad!"

"Well, you just asked, and I told you, didn't I? You've never asked before."

"Because I didn't think to ask!" I said. "Sometimes I don't know the right questions to ask, Rachel!" And as I said it I thought about my conversations with Frances, and the conversation I'd tried to have with Mum. I still didn't know how to ask about the things I needed to know. "There are some things you just have to be told!" I said.

"That's true, Ana," Rachel said. "If I knew the right questions to ask, then maybe I'd know what's going on with you. Because I know something's not right. I'm worried and I don't know what to do."

I imagined what I might say to her:

"I'm not your daughter, not completely."

"You don't feel like my real mum."

"You don't know who I am at all."

It was cruel – all of it. It would ruin her, to hear me say it. I couldn't say it. I couldn't say anything.

"Well?" Rachel said. She looked desperate.

I stood up and put my empty mug in the sink.

"I'm going back to bed. I'm tired," I said.

"Ana?" Rachel said as I went. "Don't shut me out. Please don't do that."

And I nodded and said, "Okay," because I did want to try, and because despite everything, despite my anger and my fear and my frustration, I remembered that I loved her. And I reminded myself that I shouldn't forget it.

I went upstairs and lay down on my bed.

I closed my eyes.

And I saw…Mum…standing over me, by the wall at number 38. I was hiding behind the bins in the front garden next to the wall with the rough-cut petal shapes. I was hiding from Catherine, and Dad, and from Frances, and from what I'd seen. And Mum was standing over me. She was telling me to come out from behind the bins, to come to her now, or I'd be in big trouble, and it was dark, and I couldn't quite see her face, but I knew she was angry.

"Come out of there. Now, Emma! Get out!" she was shouting.

I didn't move.

"What are you doing? Get out from behind the bins!" She was screaming now.

I didn't want to get out.

I didn't want to stop hiding.

I wanted to stay in my hiding place for ever.

"Emma! Just get up!" she screamed and when I didn't come, she reached down and grabbed me by the arm, and it hurt as she yanked me hard up off the ground. And then she bent down towards me and she said, "I need you to come with me. Just come now!" And I knew she was angry with me. I knew I had done wrong. I knew I was in the biggest trouble I could ever be in, in the whole wide world. And she dragged me back into the warm light and the humming noise of the party, and she sat me down in the corner of the room. "Stay there," she said, and I could see she was about to start crying. "Don't move!"

I sat and I tried not to think about Catherine and how I'd left her at the river – and how I'd done and seen such horrible and ugly things – and how I would be punished once they all found out what I'd done.

It was only a matter of time before they knew.

It was only a matter of time.

I hated myself for what I had done.

28.

This morning, before school, I lay down on the roof and imagined a time when I might slip again, because I could not get the feeling of falling out of my mind.

I don't know why. I was surprised that something that happened so quickly and so quietly could make me feel that way. But it did.

I wanted to reach out and grasp my fall again as I lay there.

I wondered, if I lay still and quietly enough, could I do that? Grasp it?

Because I wanted to feel it again, to give in to it.

To fall – light, weightless – where I was the space and the space was me.

29.

I just about made it through the day. Until last period. Geography.

I was meant to be writing up notes on the Richter scale. I was meant to get an A in geography. I was meant to get As in a few subjects. All these "meant to"s in life and none of them seemed relevant any more. Not when all I had in my mind was Catherine's face, and her hair, and the way it fanned out as she floated in the dark waters, and her body like a little leaf in the swollen river. I could see her now, floating, motionless, and her body filling, filling, filling with the weight of the water. She was staring back at me, and in my mind she carried on floating… She went down the river and all the way out to the grand sea… I saw her body hit the horizon… I saw myself waving in the squinting brightness of the sun as she slipped over the line… Catherine…gone… She was gone…

"Ana Ross! Are you awake over there?"

I'd fallen asleep. I'd been dreaming.

I heard Mrs Fry's voice, calling me, asking me whether I was going to take part in the class today, and I heard myself reply and tell her I was, and then I think she left me alone. I wasn't sure though, because I felt as if I kept slipping momentarily into sleep.

I shook my head. My eyes wouldn't focus and my mind just wasn't giving me any kind of a break; it was full of images almost all of the time. They were churning, spinning, repeating over and over. I thought I might pass out, but I didn't. I couldn't. However tired I was, I seemed to always be conscious.

I wished that I could sleep.

And that I could forget.

But I didn't know how to do these things any more. I couldn't control what was going through my mind, and all I could feel was the pain because of what I had done.

The bell went.

Mrs Fry turned her back on the class, and chair legs scraped the floor. The sound of it made me wince. I stared into space and I didn't move. I was just too tired to move.

"Ana!"

I heard my name being called. The sound of it broke my stare.

I looked over to the classroom door, where the voice was coming from.

Jamie.

I smiled.

Seeing him grounded me, almost instantly.

I stood up and walked over to him and he took both my hands in his, low, between us, so no one could see.

"Library?" he said.

I nodded, letting go of his hands. "But I need food, snacks, sugar!"

"Okay," he said. "Let's go."

We went to the shop and bought chocolate and cans of drink, and I fed myself fast, sitting on the park wall just up from school.

"How was your day?" I said, breaking off a fat chunk of chocolate and cramming it into my mouth.

"Fine," he said. "Better now, for seeing you."

I looked at the floor.

I could feel his eyes were still on me.

"That's nice," I said. And I looked back up at him. "That's about the nicest thing..." I broke off, afraid I might cry, but before I could Jamie bent down and he kissed me gently on the lips.

It was a tender kiss.

"Are you okay?" he said, holding my face now in his hands. "You look upset."

"No," I said. "No, I'm fine."

I took a deep breath.

"I just didn't sleep last night," I said. "I'm a bit all over the place..."

"Shall we head back to the library?"

"Sure," I said and as we walked, I felt so happy. It was pure joy that Jamie liked me so much.

When we got back to the school library it was busy. We found a table with two spaces, but they weren't next to each other. We sat down anyway, and I smiled across at him and he winked back at me as we began to get out our books.

I bent down over my geography textbook as if I was reading, and I let my hair fall over my face slightly and closed my eyes.

I thought that perhaps, if I kept still, with my eyes closed and my head down, I might eventually fall into sleep. Maybe no one would notice me either. I so wanted to sleep now. I was desperate for it. I needed it to envelop me, to close me down and rest me, and it almost did. Until I saw Catherine's body again, slipping over the horizon, and the sun going with it and there was darkness and it was all around. I wanted to open my eyes, to get away from it, and yet part of me wanted to stay – to give in to it – to see what would happen. And in those next few seconds I saw blue flashing lights, small groups of people turned inwards to one another, and a huddle of encircling arms all around. There was moaning, weeping. It was grief. And it was like a cloak gathering everyone who was there into a perpetual night.

I opened my eyes before I sunk any further.

The bright lights above the table in the library scorched my sight.

I squinted to look and find Jamie again.

"I've got to go," I whispered across to him.

"We've just got here!" he said.

"I can't concentrate. I can't think. I just—"

"Okay," he said. "Let's go." And he nodded and zipped up his bag.

We stood up together, to leave.

We got out of the school grounds and walked up to the end of the road. Jamie took my hand again and turned towards me.

"What shall we do?" he said, hitching his bag higher up onto his back. "Do you want to go home? Get some sleep?"

"I don't know," I said, looking at him. I needed to sleep, but I didn't want to leave him. Not yet.

"We could go back to yours?" he said.

I checked the time on my watch. Rachel would be home. She always got back early on a Friday.

"We could..." I said.

"What is it?"

"It's just Rachel might be in."

"So?" he said. "You don't want to come to mine – it's like a madhouse."

I'd been round to his a couple of times before. Last term, before Ellie had gone to the States and Zak and Hannah had got together. We'd all just hung out round his and watched a DVD and got pizzas. I knew what he meant. His house was full of people. He had an older brother and a younger sister, and his mum and dad seemed to always be around. I thought it was fun. It couldn't have been more different to mine. It was quiet at mine. It was totally and utterly quiet all of the time.

"I'd rather go to yours – if that's okay," I said.

"Really?" he said.

"Really."

"Okay," he said. "If you're sure."

"I'm sure," I said, smiling. Because I didn't want him to come to mine. Not yet. I didn't want to have to share him with anyone yet. And I turned in towards him and squeezed his hand, and we began to walk, and, just for a moment, I almost completely forgot about Catherine.

saturday

30.

It had been four days since Frances had called me. "You'll visit, when you've spoken to Amanda." That was the last thing she'd said to me, and still I hadn't been back to see her. I wondered what things would have been like if I'd never seen her that day in the hospital. If I hadn't recognized her like I did. I think I would have been walking around the rest of my life pretending I was normal, or a version of normal anyway, and I might just have got away with it.

Instead, right now, I was too tired to pretend. And I felt so far from normal, because I just felt so much. Feelings were coursing through me like a drug – fast and dirty – and somehow, even though I hadn't slept, I was awake. I was awake, all the time. Thinking and feeling, all the time. And my feelings were eating me raw. I was raw right down to the marrow in the deepest cracks and crevices of my bones. I had to go and see Frances. I had to. She'd asked me to go after I'd seen Mum, and I'd only seen Mum because of her.

I owed her now, in so many ways.

I got to The Avenue and knocked hard on Frances's door.

She answered.

"Hi, Frances," I said. "Can I—?"

"Ana!" she said. "Come in!" Her voice was lighter than it normally was.

She walked through to the sitting room and she was strong on her feet, moving more quickly than I'd seen before.

I closed the door and called through from the hall as I hung up my coat.

"Do you want me to put the kettle on?"

"No, no. I've just made a pot," she said. "Get yourself a mug from the kitchen and come on through."

I went to the kitchen and took a mug out the cupboard. I wondered what had put her in such a good mood. I'd never seen her like this before. When I walked into the sitting room, the answer was there.

A man stood by the fireplace. He had his back to me, his hands in his pockets.

She had a visitor.

I had this feeling suddenly, like I shouldn't be there, in the house, like I'd intruded.

I looked at Frances.

Was she going to introduce us?

She smiled. "So!" she said, clasping her hands together.

"So…" the man repeated.

And then he sighed.

And in that sigh I recognized the man.

He turned.

My dad.

It was my dad.

Standing in front of me.

And when he turned to face Frances, and saw me, his face twisted with irritation and pain.

He looked away as soon as he had seen me.

"I was just leaving," he said, quickly taking his hands out of his pockets.

His hair was grey – no, silver – like thread, and his eyes were sunken, but he was still Dad.

"No, you weren't," said Frances sharply. "You just got here, Richard. Now sit down."

And he did. He did exactly as Frances told him to.

My heart started beating, loud.

I went to introduce myself, to explain who I was. "I'm—"

"I know who you are," he said.

He wouldn't look at me.

It was strange. Here was the man who had been my dad, but I didn't have that immediate rush of love, like when I'd seen Mum. I didn't know why. I'd loved my dad, I really had.

"Sit down then, Ana. Pass me your mug." I too did as I was told.

I looked at Frances. She was so confident. She almost sparkled in Dad's company. It was like she was visibly twinkling.

She methodically poured the tea into three mugs, then the milk, and offered around a sugar bowl.

"So…you came to see Frances?" I said. I couldn't believe that he was here – still here – all these years on.

"Did you set this up, Fran?" Dad asked, ignoring me completely.

"She didn't," I said, interrupting.

I didn't like being ignored. I didn't like what he was doing to Mum, by being here.

"She didn't know I was coming," I said.

"It's true, Richard. I didn't." Frances turned to me. "In fact, I've been wondering when you were going to come, Ana. I had hoped to see you before now."

"Another strange coincidence, is it, then?" Dad said with an angry sarcasm in his voice.

"I didn't mean to do it…" I said.

The words just fell out of my mouth.

"What?" he said, now looking at me properly, for the first time.

I met his gaze, head on, and when I did, I knew why I didn't have that same feeling about him, why I didn't instantly recognize him as the dad that had swung me endlessly on our swing, tickled me until I cried, taught me how to tie my shoelaces. It was because he didn't look like the same man. He wasn't just old – he was broken.

"To hurt you – so much," I said.

I thought I was going to cry, as I said it, but I didn't.

"I'm not sure I know what you mean," he said, slower, less angry, and I saw his face younger, smiling, looking at me like he loved me – and I so wanted him to love me. Just me.

"Why did you come today, Richard?" Frances asked.

"I'm not sure I really know," he said, staring into his mug.

"And Amanda?"

"She doesn't know I'm here," he said.

"Nothing changes," said Frances, and it made me feel sick to hear her talk like that.

"So you are still together. You and –" I paused – "Amanda." The word "Amanda" felt alien in my mouth. I so wanted to say the word "Mum"; to call her Mum.

"We're still married," he said. "If that's what you mean."

"This is a happy coincidence!" said Frances. "You both being here today!" And she clapped her hands like a child. I'd never seen her behave like this before.

"I can't say that I agree," said Dad.

"You should talk to her, Richard," said Frances. "We all should."

"Why?" said Dad.

"She has come to us for a reason, I'm sure of it." Frances was talking to Dad as if I wasn't in the room. "I've been searching for an answer for so long. And she came. Not Catherine, but Emma. And of course this involves us all. It involves you too now, because it is your daughter who came. It is Emma."

"There are no answers, Frances," said Dad. "What happened has to be left alone." And he stepped back, away from us, his voice far louder than it had been before. I'd forgotten how tall he was, how lean.

He put his mug on the mantelpiece and it made a clank as he did. The noise of it echoed. And I saw him stood there, younger again, smiling, handsome. He was holding a glass of wine in his hand and his eyes were hungry for Frances. I understood that look now. And he ignored me. He shoved me out of the room and he told me to go and play on the Green. To take Catherine and to go and play on the Green.

"I don't think what happened *can* be left alone…" I said. "Not now I'm here."

I stood up, as if to meet him.

I wanted to go to him.

"I'm not interested in what you have to say," he said, finally looking at me now. "I don't know who you are, and I don't care who you think you might be. You know nothing about any of this. Nothing."

"But I do… I know loads. Loads more than I want to—"

"No one can know! No one can!" he interrupted, his voice still raised. And he came towards me, his face close – too close – to mine. I could feel the heat of his anger. It was rising up, seeping out through his pores like poison. It was directed at me. It was for me. Only me.

I drew in some air and filled my lungs and I answered back, like I was his daughter again.

"But I know!" I said. "Maybe no one else can know, but *I* know!"

"And you really expect me to believe *that*?" he said, and the harshness of his words and his body towering over me made me move back towards the sofa. I could see him standing over Mum – she was crying and he was saying he was going to leave and that he had no choice.

"Richard, calm down." Frances was on her feet now, moving towards Dad, her voice like her body, strong. "Please – don't be like this," she said and I turned to look at her because I couldn't believe what I was hearing; there was kindness in her voice, and she was softer.

"Like what?" Dad said, stepping back, away from me

and away from Frances too now, rubbing his face with his hands.

It was his hurt – his raging hurt – that was making him act like this. I tried to make myself believe it, to remember, to understand.

I took another deep breath – and with it came a flutter of memories like paper blowing on the wind.

"You bought me Doublemint chewing gum every time we went to fill the car up with petrol. You used to drop it through the sunroof. I'd wait for it, every time. You'd walk towards the car, like you had nothing in your hands, no treats, nothing, and then as you went to open the car door you'd drop it onto my lap from above, and I'd squeal with delight."

Dad didn't say anything. But he kept looking at me. I could tell he wanted more.

"I used to clean the car with you. On a Sunday. You'd wax and polish and I'd take a washing-up bowl full of soapy water and an old toothbrush and I'd scrub the wheel hubs until the silver metal shone."

"What colour was it? The car?" he said.

"Red," I said. "Red with a black stripe along the sides."

"Where did we live?" he said, questioning me.

"Here," I said. "The Avenue. Number 42." I glanced at Frances as I said it. Her face was utterly still. She didn't for one second give me away.

"Where did I work? What did I do?" Dad asked.

"I don't know... I don't know where it was. I don't know what you did..." I said. I was desperate not to lose this conversation. "I...I was just a child... I didn't know... I was just a child."

He sat down and dropped his head into his hands, his neat suit hiding his crumpled body.

I looked at Frances. I didn't know what to do – whether to go on talking. She looked at me and nodded.

"Go to him," she whispered, but I could sense that she wanted to go to him too. We both felt it: his need. I wanted to touch his back, to comfort him, and Frances – well, I think she wanted to hold him, be tender, to mend him. But neither of us moved, silently allowing the other to take the opportunity to go to him. Then as she went over to him, I spoke:

"Dad, I..."

He looked up. And he scowled. His face was distorted with it – an expression I wished never to see again – a mixture of tortured confusion and anger and horrified disbelief. And I'd put it there. And somehow I knew it wasn't the first time that I'd done it.

And he left.

The front door slammed, and Frances stood alone, her arm suspended in mid-air where he had been, and the word "Dad" left hanging like a solitary and desperate unanswered cry for help...

My phone rang.

I looked at my watch. It was three o'clock. I scrabbled around in my bag for the phone, glad of the distraction it provided.

Frances bent down and picked the tray up from the coffee table and headed out to the kitchen.

One missed call. Jamie. It was Saturday. I guessed he was ringing to see if I wanted to meet him tonight. I wanted to call him straight back, but I needed to speak to Frances first, tell her about Mum. That was why I'd come.

A text came through.

How about I come to yours? For 6pm? Jx

I didn't want him to come to mine, not yet, but I couldn't think of anything better to suggest, and I really wanted to see him, so I texted straight back.

Yes. OK. Ax

I dumped my phone in my bag and went into the kitchen to speak to Frances.

She was moving around like a fish darting between the

reeds: lithe and quick. I stood and watched her for a minute.

"You're better," I said.

"Today," she said. "It goes like that sometimes."

There was a silence.

"Did you know he was coming?" I asked.

"He called – an hour before he arrived," she said.

"It didn't go very well. I—"

"No," she said. "No, it didn't."

"I thought...I almost thought I'd..."

"Convinced him?" Frances said, now turning to look at me.

"Well, yes," I said. "Is there something wrong in that?"

Frances's voice sounded harder again, like before.

"You *are* taking this seriously, aren't you, Ana?" she said. "These are real lives you are dealing with here. We – all of us – have real lives, you know."

"I know that," I said. "Why do you say that?"

I could feel the beginnings of her anger rising. All the softness in her voice had gone. I wanted to stop her changing. To stop her anger. I wanted the lighter voice back, the one she'd had before, when Dad was here. The voice that didn't frighten me so much. But I could only hear the voice that I remembered from before – and I could hear it now – and I could hear it as I'd heard it then—

"You!" she'd said.

My shoes were wet from the river. There were people all around us in the darkness. Police were putting tape across the road and around the Green. Frances's voice was so clear and cold it made me shiver.

"I saw you!" she said. "I saw you!"

And I felt a panic rising up inside me, fast and urgent, and I thought I'd be sick with the guilt and the shame.

I looked up at her as she stood in the kitchen now.

"What is it, Ana?"

"Nothing," I said, my heart racing. She'd been softer, kinder, with Dad, but that Frances was not the Frances I knew. The Frances I knew was cruel and hard, and her change of mood now was everywhere in the room, like an infection; it was crawling the walls.

She turned away from me, back to the sink, to start tidying up.

"I said I'd come back when I'd spoken to Mum," I said.

She didn't reply.

"You asked me to come," I said.

"I know I did," Frances said and she carried on putting things away, swiftly, with ease. It was as if seeing Richard had greased the joints of her decaying bones.

"It was amazing," I said. "To see her, to hug her, to just talk."

"I can only imagine," Frances said, and she stopped what she was doing and she looked directly at me. "It seems so wrong to me," she said, "that you have a reunion, and I don't."

"I..." My voice slipped, cracked away from me.

"So will you see her again?" Frances said.

"I want to, but—"

"We should meet. All of us. Together."

I felt unsure. I didn't answer.

"I want to know why you are here, Ana. I want to make sense of it. I believe we can only do that together," she said.

"Surely no one can know why I'm here."

"You must have come to me for a reason," Frances said. "You must have. I realize that now. I have been searching for the answers for so long, and you came. You! Emma! I just need to decide what I must do now you are here."

"Do?" I said. "There is nothing to do! I am just here," I said. "I just am."

"So what did Amanda say, about Catherine – I assume you asked?" Frances said.

"She said she wouldn't talk about it."

"What did she say – exactly?"

"That she wouldn't talk about it, about that night, about Catherine. And then she told me that Dad wouldn't see me."

"Ah, but he has!" said Frances. She was pleased with that, somehow. "And we *will* meet," she said. "All of us. Trust me. It will happen."

31.

When I got home from Frances's I went straight up onto the roof.

There was no sun.

I lay on the roof and the cold crept into my bones like a tide. Still, I stayed. Quietly I lay. So that I could look up into the wide expanse of the sky.

And I thought about how, if I could, I would pull all the badness out of me. I would pull it out of me like a long, wet, heavy rope, and I would drop it down the side of this building, and let it gather on the pavement in a coil.

It would make an ugly ring

One wet layer lying on top of the other.

And I would leave it there.

I would walk away, and leave it there, to rot.

My rotting guilt.

And then I would be free.

I would be free.

32.

Grillie came over that night. I had no idea she was coming. She started talking to me as soon as I got down the stairs.

"Your mother's in the bath. I won't eat pizza, so we're having salmon cutlets and baked potatoes," she said.

Jamie was going to be here soon. There was no way I could stop him meeting the whole family now. My heart sank at the thought of it.

"I didn't know you'd be here tonight, Grillie," I said.

"Grown-ups can have secrets too, you know," she said and she winked at me. "Come here and give your Grillie a hug." And as I did I thought about Frances – about Grillie and Frances – and I worried that Grillie might know more than I wanted her to.

"You look tired," she said.

"I'm okay," I said, shaking my head, shaking her concern away.

"I believe you," Grillie said. "I'm not sure if I should, but I do."

I felt myself blush. I never normally blushed.

"Now," she said. "Sit down. I want to talk to you about something. Before Rachel gets out of the bath."

I went and sat next to her on the sofa. I braced myself for what she might say.

"You haven't been over in a while," she said.

"I know, I'm sorry..." I'd totally messed up. I used to be around Grillie's all the time. We'd play Scrabble and eat chocolate biscuits. But that was before.

"You don't need to say sorry. Life changes, you're growing up – I understand," she said. "But what I don't understand is why you go and see Frances Wells."

"Frances?" I said. It was completely obvious I was playing for time. I swallowed. The noise of it was loud in my ears.

"You know who I mean," she said. "Frances Wells. The woman in the hospital. I've played bridge with her a couple of times now. She's joined our club."

I nodded.

"She sees you more than I do these days," Grillie said.

The doorbell went. Jamie. I didn't know what to say, but I couldn't go and get the door until I gave Grillie some kind of an answer.

"It's complicated," I said.

It was all I could think to say.

"Can I give you some advice?" Grillie said. "Sometimes

it doesn't have to be. Sometimes we make it more complicated than it needs to be." And she put her hand over my hand and patted it, where it sat on the arm of the sofa, and she smiled. "You know I'll always love you, Ana – no matter what you do."

I looked at her face – it was full of love and kind gentleness. I was glad that she had come. It was comforting, to have seen her.

The doorbell went again.

"You'd better get that," she said. "Don't want to keep whoever it is waiting."

Rachel invited Jamie to stay for dinner, and he stayed.

And we actually had a great dinner. I'm not sure why I was so surprised that we did. I mean, whatever I thought about Rachel, when it came down to it she was a pretty cool parent, and I think lately I'd forgotten that.

Grillie told us why she didn't like pizza, why she wouldn't eat it under any circumstances. She believed too much dough wasn't good for a person. That it filled you up, made you bloated. She said it had made her stomach so bloated once she thought she'd actually lift off the ground and fly away. And she talked about how the recipe for the salmon cutlets had been passed down from mother to daughter all the way through five generations, and how no one made those cutlets like her own mother.

"The pressure's on then!" Jamie said, smiling at me and Rachel, and Grillie squealed and clapped her hands with joy.

"I like this boy!" she said, slapping him on the back. "I like him!" And I was pleased.

By the end of the meal Grillie had a captivated audience in Jamie, and she didn't show any signs of letting up. Jamie didn't seem in the least bit bored. He was enjoying himself, I could see that. So was I, but I was desperate to take him away from Grillie and pull him into my room, so we could be on our own. I kept trying to give him a sign, but short of actually dragging him away from the table I wasn't sure what I could do. And my eyes were becoming heavy with the need for sleep now.

Grillie was on a complete roll with the story of how she and Grandad Bob got together. I'd never got to meet Grandad Bob but I'd heard so much I felt like I had. Grillie loved telling stories about him – always in the exact same way, laughing in the exact same places – and I loved them too, but all I wanted to do was be with Jamie.

Rachel spoke. "Come on, Mum. Let's make some coffee."

"I'm enjoying myself!" said Grillie, like a petulant child. "Don't stop me enjoying myself!" And she laughed conspiratorially with Jamie, who at last stood up and showed signs that he was ready to make a move from the table.

"Ana, do you want to watch a DVD? You could watch it in your room," Rachel said, clearing the table.

"Yes, yes," I said. I couldn't hide the astonishment from my face; Rachel had actually orchestrated this getaway for me.

She walked over and handed me a DVD.

"I was young and in love myself once upon a time, you know…" she whispered so Jamie couldn't hear, and then she walked back towards the kitchen, swiping a tea towel off the table as she went.

"Grillie is great," Jamie said, flopping back on my bed and kicking his shoes off. I had my back to him as I loaded the DVD into the player.

"She is," I said, "but I thought we'd never get out of there!" And I turned round and sat down next to him, close, and I kissed him. I'd waited all evening to kiss him like that again, and it felt strong, different.

"I missed you," I said.

"But I haven't been anywhere," said Jamie, smiling.

"I know," I said, "but still, I missed you."

sunday

33.

I must have slept that night. I'd gone to bed after Jamie left and I must have slept because I remember waking up.

I'd woken and stayed in bed staring at the ceiling, watching the clock turn through the hours – 1 a.m., 2 a.m., 3 a.m. – and then it was 7 a.m., so I must have slept some more. And I woke then because my heart was racing and I was wet through. The sheets were cold underneath me, my pyjamas damp. I ran my hand across my chest and wiped off hundreds of tiny beads of sweat.

"I saw you!" she said. "I saw you!"

Panic gripped me, as it had then. Frances. She'd seen me. I'd been seen. I felt sick with them knowing what I did.

I swallowed.

And still, I didn't remember.

Why didn't I remember?

I needed her to tell me. To say it. Because not remembering, and feeling this way, not sleeping this way, the guilt and the shame, it was like some parasite was eating me from the inside out.

Today was Sunday.

I would go and see Frances.

And I would ask her to tell me what she'd seen.

I'd ask her to tell me it all.

Because she had seen.

She must have seen it all.

I banged on Frances's door.

There was no answer.

I waited a few moments, and I knocked again.

Nothing.

I walked into the front garden and I looked through the windows into the sitting room. There were things out on the coffee table – signs of life; she was home. I decided I would wait.

I turned back and walked to the front door and stood in the porch.

I had stood in the porch the night Catherine died. My feet so wet and muddy from the river, my throat so taut and dry it hurt. The police were stood at Frances's gate by the front wall, and I was meant to have gone inside the house. Mum was coming. The police were going to ask us both some questions. They wanted me in the house, away from all the chaos outside. That's what one of them said. "Can we take her in here, just until my colleagues arrive? She can go home with the mother for questioning after that." I'd stood in the porch looking for Mum, willing her to come, and suddenly Frances was there. She was towering over me in the doorway – shouting at me –

"I saw you! I saw you!"

I could see Mum in the street now, talking, crying, arguing with Dad. He went to stroke her arm and she pushed him away. I wanted to call for my mum, but I couldn't. Because Frances was standing over me, blocking me from sight, boxing me in towards the front door. I wanted to get away, to get to my mum, but I couldn't, and all the time Frances was saying over and over –

"She's dead! She's dead! She's gone! Because of you! How could you? We trusted you, and she's gone."

And then a policewoman came and started to talk to Frances. She took her away from me and into the hall. I was relieved. But Frances was still shouting and I made myself block out her words, her anger. I just kept looking for Mum…until I was shoved… Frances came past me in the porch and walked quickly, urgently out of the house, through the front garden and into the street towards Mum and Dad.

I felt a tightening in my chest. Air was slowly seeping out of me like a deflating balloon. I gasped and gasped… I tried to catch my breath… I willed for it to come through my panic and then I heard a sound, behind me—

"Ana?"

I turned towards the voice.

It was the same voice.

Frances.

I was present, again.

She was standing at the front door.

I pulled in a breath. My body pulsed with the need for it, the satisfaction of gaining it.

"Come in," Frances said, and she beckoned me into the house.

I took myself into the sitting room and sat down. My legs were shaking.

"What is it, Ana?" Frances said. "You're shaking."

"I need you to tell me," I said.

"Tell you what?"

"What I did. How it happened. How I killed her."

Frances didn't speak.

Suddenly I knew I couldn't do this without Mum. I had to have my mum.

"Have they agreed to come here, Mum and Dad?" I said. "I want to be here, when they come."

"You need to be, Ana," Frances said. "I'm glad that you see that now."

I didn't speak.

"You know I'm not doing any of this for you, Ana," she said. "This has never been about you. I'm doing this for Catherine. Only Catherine."

Hearing Catherine's name in that moment hit me like a physical blow. I could feel my heart racing again, and my body began to twitch involuntarily.

"You came to me – you wanted to know about Catherine," Frances went on. "You wanted to talk. I said I would talk to you – but that is all – that is all I will ever do for you—"

"I know I killed her!" I screamed. "But why don't I remember what I did?"

"You didn't remember the house you were born in, Ana. You needed to come to me. That's why you are here." Frances was so calm.

"No!" I said. "I'm here because I saw you…at the hospital…and when I saw you…the memories…they came back to me…more of them… I mean, I'd always known I was Emma – that I had been Emma…always. I'm used to it now – or I was – until I saw you two weeks ago and I started to remember things I'd never remembered before, and feel things I'd never felt before. Dreadful things. Things that keep me awake at night because I feel so bad about what I've done. You will never know, Frances, how bad I feel – and I wish I could explain it, so you'd know. But I can't…words can never be enough…or say enough…and I can't pull out my feelings and show them to you – to prove what I say is true – that I'm sorry… I'm so sorry for what I did. Please – just tell me what happened – so I can remember what I did – so I can know the truth – there is no one else – I have no one else I can ask—"

"Ah, the truth!" Frances said. "That can be an elusive thing, don't you think?"

"No!" I said. "No!" But I was no longer sure what I was saying back to her, or what she was saying to me. Her words were slow and jumbled; it felt as if I was slipping slowly into sleep. I leaned forwards to try and listen – harder, better.

"I would say that what you remember, and what you feel, are two very different things, aren't they, Ana?"

"What?"

"You say you don't remember what you did, but you know how bad you felt when you did it – because you know what you did – you know."

"I don't remember!" I said.

"I never got to speak to you after that day – the day she died. They didn't let me see you," Frances said.

"If I did it, if I pushed her, if I dragged her in there, why don't I remember?" I said, and as I said the words I could feel my pulse speeding up, pounding in my neck, my wrists, my groin, at every pressure point, like a drum roll gaining speed; my head began to throb. I needed to stand up again. I wanted to stand up.

I walked towards the fireplace.

I held on to the mantelpiece.

Dad's mug was still there from yesterday; his half-drunk cup of tea sat with a thin film across the top of it, the milk cloudy where it had soured, and a dirty ring clinging to the inside of the mug.

I couldn't take my eyes off it.

Frances hadn't touched it. She hadn't moved it. She had left his mug in the place where he had last been.

I closed my eyes.

And I saw Mum coming towards me.

I was sat in the corner at the party, just as she'd left me.

"I've been back to Frances's and I've seen Dad. I've told him you're here, with me," she said and her voice wavered as she spoke.

And I saw Dad and Frances again, on the stairs.

Dad kissing Frances.

"Where is Catherine, Emma? Do you know where Catherine is?" Mum said.

I shook my head.

"Because she's not at Frances's. Dad says you two were playing together, out on the Green. Is that right?"

I nodded.

"So where is she, Emma? It's very important that you

tell me. It's dark outside. She's only six. We need to find her."

I nodded again.

"Will you show me where you were playing?"

I nodded, and I bit my lip and I tasted blood but I sucked it away so Mum wouldn't see.

And she took my hand and she walked me out of the house and into the darkness on the Green and I was scared. Because now they would know. They would all know what I had done.

I opened my eyes.

I looked up at Frances and again at the mug on the mantelpiece. Dad's mug.

"You still love him," I said. "You still love Dad."

"I was only nineteen years old when I married Al," she said, looking straight ahead of her, her gaze fixed on a point out of the window. "Our fathers worked together. He lived three streets away. It wasn't an arranged marriage, as such – not like you'd understand an arranged marriage today – but it felt like one."

"Why are you telling me this?" I said. I didn't move. I traced the patterns over and over on the carpet and I counted in my head as I did it, to try and keep myself focused, to try and keep myself in the room.

"When Catherine was born, everything changed for me. I loved her. And everything was better in the world.

When you know what it is to love a person, unconditionally, that's how it makes you feel, don't you think?"

I nodded.

I knew that was how Rachel felt about me.

"You see, I loved Catherine, and I loved Richard," she said. "I never loved Al, not really. Perhaps that's why we never had a child."

I felt a sickness building up inside me.

I wanted to cry, but I couldn't. Instead I counted. I kept counting, in my head, waiting for the tears to come. But they wouldn't. And I couldn't swallow and I couldn't breathe. I was drowning in a pool of saltwater sorrow – it was filling my neck, my throat, and cracking as it crystallized in my ears.

"When I saw Catherine's body after she'd been pulled out of the water," Frances said, "I saw a darkness like I had never known before. *This is what it feels like to be blind*, I thought, *but to have known the gift of sight*. You see, it pressed against my eyes, and there was nothing but black, black, black...blackest black." Her voice was rising now, growing louder with every word. "After you experience that, life is forever torn. My love for Catherine was swallowed by loss long ago," she said. "But Richard – he could still remind me of what it was to love. And in him, there will always be something of Catherine," she said.

I held on to the mantelpiece and my eyes began to go again. I was weak.

I could feel my feet so wet from the river. My shoes caked in thick black mud. I wanted to stamp my feet and make the mud fall off. I wanted to get it off me. But I couldn't. It was stuck.

Mum was coming towards the house now. It was so dark, but it was her. I could see by her walk, her outline. She had left Dad behind her in the street and she was walking towards me. At last.

"Mum!" I screamed out to her, and the policewoman put one hand on my shoulder, to stop me from going to her, and Frances was almost at Mum now in the street.

"Emma!" shouted Mum, and Frances tried to grab Mum's arm, to try and stop her, to talk to her, and Mum pulled her arm away. "Get off me!" Mum screamed. "Don't touch me!" And she kept walking towards me.

And I knew then that Mum knew. She knew what I knew – about Dad and Frances. And I ran. Because I didn't want to talk to her about what I'd seen or what I'd done. I couldn't. So I ran. I pulled myself away from the policewoman and I ran into the house and into the sitting room, and the policewoman let me go in, she didn't follow, because that was where I was meant to be: in the house, with Mum.

I had to hide. I had to find a place in the house where no one could find me. I ran into the sitting room. I could hear Dad outside shouting for Mum, and for Frances, and they were all coming now, following me into the house. They were all coming for me. I stood in front of the fireplace, unsure which way to go. I'd done something so bad, so very bad, and all I wanted to do was hide but I couldn't move. The voices outside were getting nearer: Mum, Frances, Dad, the police—

"GET OUT!" Frances shouted as she walked into the room.

Mum was stood looking at me.

"BOTH OF YOU! GET OUT OF MY HOUSE! JUST GET OUT!" Frances was screaming now. I could hear Dad's footsteps as he came through the front door. He was calling for Mum. He'd be here, in the room, any second.

I was sobbing now.

I could hardly breathe.

"Emma, come here," Mum said, reaching her hand out towards me. "Come to me."

"Get her out, Amanda!" said Frances. "Get her out! Now!"

Dad was in the doorway.

He stood still.

"Richard! Do something!" screamed Frances, turning to Dad. "Take Emma! Get her out! I don't want to see her! I can't look at her!"

"I didn't mean to do it," I sobbed. "I didn't mean to—"

"Amanda, you should take her," Dad said, looking at Mum. He was slow, calm.

"And leave you here? With Frances?" Mum said.

"I need him here, Amanda," Frances said. "He needs to be here with me tonight."

I shook my head to stop myself from passing out, and I opened my eyes.

The memory was so strong it was moving me, physically; I felt sick, and I was shaking. I didn't want to feel this way. I tried to bring myself back into the moment. Had I momentarily fallen out of consciousness? I couldn't tell. I was shaking. I couldn't stop myself shaking. It felt like there was nothing to grasp on to any more.

I looked at Frances's face – her old, worn face.

"What are you saying, Frances?" I said. "I don't understand what you are saying. What do you mean, in him there will always be something of Catherine?"

I could hear Mum screaming now.

"*We* need him, Frances!"

That night – the memory – with me again.

"Look at her! At Emma! Look at her, Richard!" Mum said. "She doesn't know what's going on! She's just a child. She doesn't understand. She's scared. I'm scared. Richard, you need to be with us. With me and with Emma – with *us*."

I remember I gagged.

I gagged again – now.

"What I'm saying, Ana," Frances said, "is that Catherine was our child – mine and Richard's. She was your sister. I told you, the night that she died. You needed to know. You had a right to know. She was your sister."

I fell to the floor.

I felt my legs go, and I opened my mouth to cry out, but I knew I was going to hit the floor and there was nothing I could do about it.

I heard the hollow thud of my head hitting the iron grate in the fireplace, and a strike of pain shot through me like an electric current.

The last thing I saw was the fire stand flying into the centre of the room; the poker and bellows and the shovel, mid-air, making a cacophony of sound as they went. And Frances. Immobile. Watching me fall.

34.

I am floating. I am sitting on a shard of ice and I am floating on an endless sea. The sea is like a glass pool. It reflects only the whiteness all around, and it cannot be cracked or broken. There is stillness everywhere. I am cold and wet. My skin, my clothes, all of me aches with the cold. And the sun is bright, but I can feel no heat. There is just white light. And now...now there is the sound of breathing. Behind me. It's gentle at first. It brings me warmth...a heavy warmth. And it closes in on me... I need that warmth, but I know it's not good.

It's my polar bear.

I know it is.

He's back.

And I don't want to turn around because he will be close, closer than I want him to be, and I don't know whether he is my friend any more.

Maybe if I don't turn around to face him, he'll leave.

But he doesn't leave, and I know, from the shape of his

shadow, that he is on his hind legs, getting ready to take me… Still I can feel the warmth of his breath. I look up. So I can see him one last time. And it *is* him. And as his face leans down towards me I think about how I knew it was him. How I knew him. How I knew his breath, and now, his long body and his strong open jaw as he comes towards me. And I know what he will do to me and I am glad. Because when he takes me I will be dispersed, and in that there may be more than just some momentary peace. In that there may be a forever peace.

35.

I came to exactly where I had landed when I fell. Frances was still in her chair. I could feel a dampness on my face. I reached up. There was a wet flannel on my forehead. Pain was throbbing above my ear. I moved my hand from the flannel to my head – my hair was warm and wet and sticky. Blood. I pulled my legs up towards me and used them to steady myself into a sitting position. Frances was now gazing out of the window.

"Please," I said. I started to cry. "It hurts…" I wanted her to help me. For someone to help me. So I could stand up. So I could go.

"I'm sure it does," she said, sitting utterly still.

"I need to go," I said, trying to push myself up so I could get to my feet. My head was pounding out a bass beat in my ears and my legs were shaking, but I was determined to get my bag and get out of the house.

"I'd ask someone to look at that, if I were you," Frances said.

"Yes," I said, still crying.

She followed me to the front door.

"I will see you tomorrow morning," she said. "Amanda and Richard are coming at ten."

"I have school," I said.

"I'm sure you can miss one day. It's important. You said you wanted to come."

I turned and left.

I walked up the front path and reached into my bag for my phone, and called Rachel.

"Rachel," I said, "I – I'm hurt. I need you."

"Where are you, Ana?" Rachel said. "Where are you?"

"I'm on my way – to A&E, West Middlesex," I said and I hung up because the pain in my head was so strong, and I didn't know how to explain. I couldn't think how to explain, and I just knew that Rachel would come, that she would be there, when I got to the hospital. I just knew that she would come.

36.

We sat in the hard plastic chairs in A&E waiting to be seen for what felt like several days. Around us was an assortment of injured and maimed people, and I couldn't stop myself looking at everyone. At their pain. There was so much pain. And yet Rachel seemed indifferent to it all. She only cared about me.

"So tell me again how you did this, Ana," Rachel said.

I told her that I'd fallen down the stairs at the station. That I'd gone with Hannah into Richmond, to the phone shop. I told her that it didn't hurt that much at first, when I fell, and I hadn't realized it was bleeding until I started to make my way home.

"How did you fall?"

"I just lost my footing. Tripped. I told you. One of those stupid things. It's nothing."

She lifted the hair again over my ear to take another look. She made a slight hissing noise through her teeth.

"Is it bad?" I said.

"It doesn't look that good," she said, "but you'll live."

"I'll live," I said back to her, and as I said it I looked at her, my eyes reflected in hers. "That's good, isn't it?" I said, and I felt like I might cry, but I bit my lip instead.

Rachel smiled, and stroked the back of my head with her hand, smoothing my hair into my neck. And I let her. It felt comforting, warm. I was lulled by it. "Yes, Ana. That's good," she said.

Sleep was almost there, within my reach. I went to go towards it. I was ready to give in.

"I love you so much, Ana," Rachel whispered, kissing the top of my head. "I just want everything to be okay."

"I know," I said and as I slipped further towards unconsciousness I saw Frances Wells standing outside her front door. She was screaming, crying, and Dad was trying to get her to go inside the house. Her navy dress was wet and dark where she had held Catherine's limp body against her own. There were grass and leaves from the river covering her shoes, stuck to her legs. And Dad – he had stayed with her. He'd watched as I'd been led away from the house by the police, with Mum, and he had stayed, with Frances.

"...I'll try harder," Rachel was saying, "...if that's what it takes..." and her voice melted into the pictures in my head, and I didn't know what she was saying. I'd lost all sense of conversation, all sense of time.

"Don't try anything, Rachel," I said back, only conscious of the words after I'd said them.

"What do you mean?"

"I mean – I mean – you should just be you – and I'll try and be me…"

"Ana?"

"…and well – let's see – what happens now…"

"What do you mean?" she said.

"It's not always so simple," I said. "You don't know the whole story, the whole messy messiness of me and what happened to me…" For a split second I felt myself fall into sleep and then Rachel turned and lifted my head off her shoulder and cradled my face in her hands and I was awake again.

"Tell me – what you mean – when you say that," she demanded. "What aren't you telling me? Just tell me what's going on, Ana. Please. If it's drugs or something, I need to know. You need to tell me. So I can help you. I won't be cross – just tell me – what is it?"

"I can't say it. It's complicated…" And as I said it I thought of Grillie and I burst out laughing and as I laughed tears poured out of my eyes like a gutter channelling the rains after a storm, and I thought it would never stop.

"Sit up," Rachel said. "Properly."

I looked at her. She looked like she was going to cry.

"You're not well. Really, you're not well… How do you

feel?" she asked, touching my forehead again. "I think you're concussed. I'm going to talk to them, find out how much longer it's likely to be."

"Don't go!" I cried out, as she moved off towards the desk.

She turned. "I won't be a minute," she said, but as I watched her get up and walk to the desk I willed her back to me. I needed her. I needed her so much, and the thought that she was going away from me now brought a loose uncontrolled sickness to my belly again.

I put my head between my legs.

My head was throbbing, but it didn't stop me wishing.

I hung my head low and I sat and I wished.

I wished that I might undo it – undo all that I did – and I blocked out the pain in my head – and I wished and I wished and I wished.

37.

"What are you doing? You're meant to be resting, remember?" Rachel was guiding me back to the sofa and passing me the remote control. "Watch something. I don't want you wandering about. You need to relax."

I couldn't relax. I couldn't stop thinking about Frances, and how she'd left me, by the fireplace, and how I was hurt and she didn't care. And Catherine, my half-sister, Catherine. It had all been a lie: my mum, my dad, my family. And Frances was a massive part of it. She stood between my parents and me. We were all connected. I didn't want us to be, but we were. It wasn't just the events of that night that connected us any more.

"Sit down, Ana. Please. Let me get you something to eat," Rachel said.

We'd only been back from A&E twenty minutes and she was already fussing.

"I'm not hungry."

"I'll get you a drink then," Rachel said and she walked into the kitchen.

My phone buzzed.

There was a text from Jamie.

Thinking of you, lovely Ana. See you tomorrow. Jx

I texted back two kisses. I had nothing, in that moment, to say. I felt lost. If Jamie knew what I had done he wouldn't want to call me or see me ever again.

Rachel handed me a cup of tea. "Here, drink this. Will you be okay for a bit if I go and take a shower."

"Sure."

"I won't be long," she said.

I looked at my phone again.

I pulled up Jamie's text and reread it a couple of times, then I put my phone away again, and I went upstairs and lay down on my bed.

"I'm meant to be going out tonight." Rachel appeared at my bedroom door after her shower. "But I'm going to cancel," she said, and she walked out and into her room.

I followed her in.

"Don't cancel – not for me. I'll be fine."

I went and stood behind her as she sat at her dressing table and brushed her hair, looking at herself in the mirror. She had gorgeous thick hair that bounced up in waves around the back. She called it uncontrollable. I called it luscious, which kind of annoyed her. She hated the attention. She could never take a compliment.

"I can't go," she said. "Not with you, like this."

"I'm fine," I said.

She raised her eyebrows and looked at me.

"I'm fine. Really."

"Any pain?"

"No, no pain. No chance of that with the pills they gave me," I said.

"Good," she said. "But still, I think I should stay home, in case you need me."

"Really?" I said.

"Really," she said.

I didn't want to admit it, but I was glad.

I reached out and gathered her hair in my hands and scooped it up onto the top of her head, and we both looked at her in the mirror. She was beautiful. Elegant. I stood behind her. Plain. Damaged.

"I thought Jamie was nice," she said.

"Really?" I shrugged, pretending like it was no big deal to hear her say that.

She smiled. "You okay?" she said.

I nodded, and let go of her hair.

I left it a moment, before I spoke again.

"When did you first, you know, fall in love?"

"Oh," she said. "Now there's a question!"

Our eyes met again in the mirror. I was embarrassed. But I'd asked her now.

"It was Year Seven. Ben Bolton."

"Year Seven?"

"Yup!"

"And you knew it was love?"

"I knew," Rachel said, smiling. "I put a note in his locker every day for a week. It had to be love."

"But how did you know?" I said.

"Because when I wasn't with him I could only think of him. Because when I wasn't with him I was simply waiting until I was. And when I was with him, I didn't want to be anywhere else."

I nodded again, looking at my feet.

"When it's right with someone, you just know, Ana. It's the simplest thing in the world."

"Okay," I said, as if I understood. But I didn't. I thought about Mum and Dad, and Frances and Al, and I thought about Dad and Frances. I didn't believe that all love could be as simple as Rachel had described it.

She turned around and squeezed the chub of my cheek between her forefinger and thumb like she used to when I was little; it was playful, and she seemed happy. "Don't look so worried, Ana. Everything will be okay. I promise."

And as much as I wanted to believe her, to take her

promise and hold it in the palm of my hand like it was the most precious thing on earth, I couldn't. Because I wasn't the same person I'd been two weeks ago – the person who saw the good in everything and believed in the truth. I had killed someone. I had done that. And not just anyone. I had killed my sister. My only sister. And nothing could reverse that or make it better. Surely I was here as Ana, now, to suffer in this life for what I had done. I had to be. That had to be why I was here. That had to be the reason. And the suffering, it had really only just begun.

38.

As soon as Rachel turned the hall light off that night, I climbed out of my bed and onto the roof.

The air was cool, and I was still.

No one knows I'm here, I thought.

No one needs to know that I'm here.

No one needs to know that I come to this high-up place with open edges and sloping sides. That's the whole point of this place. It's a place where no one can find me. No people, no memories, no one.

And everything that happens here is my own.

Ana's. Not Emma's. It is my own.

And if I fell off this roof…

If I slipped or rolled or let myself slide…

It would be mine.

It would be my own.

It would be totally my own.

Because I need it to be, to be Ana. I need something that is my own.

monday

39.

I slept all night. I slept like I was dead. It must have been the painkillers, but whatever it was, I didn't care. The sleep was good, and I felt better for it. Or at least I did in my first waking moments. And then Frances's voice was with me again—

"She's dead! She's dead! She's gone! Because of you! How could you? We trusted you, and she's gone."

I turned over and pulled the duvet in, closer, so it was all around me.

I was going to see Mum and Dad today. I was going back to The Avenue and I was going to see them both, together, with Frances. I was going to find out exactly what I had done.

I got up and made some breakfast. I opened up my laptop and typed a permission letter for school while I ate. I printed it off and forged Rachel's signature. It looked pretty close. It would do. I'd decided not to bunk off. I'd go in for registration and then leave. I'd put in the letter that I had a hospital appointment following up on my stitches, that I'd be back at lunchtime. I didn't want to bunk and give Rachel any more reasons to worry. She had enough reasons already.

As I walked into school I saw there was a missed call on my phone, and a message began to ring through. I stopped and walked back to the gates to pick it up.

"Ana, hello. It's Amanda – Amanda Trees. I know we're seeing each other this morning, but...I said I'd be in touch – and, I know I haven't – and, well – I found something – something I'd like you to have. I don't really want to say any more, not on the phone...but I wanted to let you know that I'll bring it today – and I'm sorry I haven't called until now – but I'll see you later. Bye now."

I looked at my phone. It was 8.40 a.m.

One hour and twenty minutes until I would see her.

I just had to get through registration.

Then I could leave.

I could see my mum.

I walked to my classroom and as I did the stitches in my head started to pull, sharply, above my ear. I took a deep breath in, to steady myself, and I put my feet down...one in front of the other...to the pulse in my head...one in front of the other to the pulse in my head...one in front of the other to the pulse in my head... I was marching to the beat of my own adrenalin.

"Hey, Ana!"

Jamie was sat on one of the tables calling me over as I came into class.

"How are you?" he said.

"Yeah, okay."

"Just okay?" he said.

"Well, apart from this." I raised my hand to my head.

"What happened?" he said.

I lifted my hair up over my ear. He put his hand on my neck as he looked, and he smoothed the skin close to my cut with his fingers. It tingled with his touch.

"I fell," I said. "It was stupid—"

Mrs Kavanagh walked in.

"Everyone sitting down for registration now please." And she started to run through the names.

As soon as the register was finished Jamie stood up and came back over to me.

"You should've called me. I'd have come over."

He took my hands gently in his.

"I was just too tired," I said as the bell sounded. "On major painkillers – look—"

"I wish you'd called me," he interrupted. "Seriously."

"I'm sorry, Jamie – I am. I didn't think—"

"What? That I'd want to know?"

"That's not what I meant – look – I'm sorry," I said and I pulled my hands out from his without looking at him – I couldn't bear to – and I ran out of class and down the corridor and out onto the street because I had to get out. I just had to get out of school and into the cooler air, and I had to get to The Avenue so I could see my mum. Because I couldn't wait any longer to see her now.

40.

I ran from the bus stop and knocked loudly on Frances's door.

"Frances," I said, when she answered.

My breath was short from running, my heart drumming, my wound throbbing. I hadn't realized I was feeling so strung out until I spoke and my voice was uneven, raspy.

"Are – they here – yet?" I said but before she could answer I bent over and put my hands on my knees, dipping my head down to stop myself passing out.

She opened the door wider. "Come in," she said. "I'll get you some water."

And she closed the door behind me.

I went into the living room. It was empty. I looked out of the window for Dad's car. The street was so quiet. I couldn't see anyone. They weren't here.

Frances was in the kitchen. I could hear all sorts of things being moved about, not just cups and cutlery, but chairs and cupboard doors, like she was arranging and rearranging things. It distracted me, but not enough to make me go into the kitchen to see what she was doing. And anyway, I didn't want to be near her. I was glad to be away from her, in another room, standing at the window, waiting for Mum and Dad.

"Your water," said Frances, suddenly behind me with a glass. She made me jump. "Are you nervous, Ana?" she said.

"No," I said, lying, turning to face her. She handed me the water. I took a sip.

"They'll be here," she said. "In a minute." And she walked back out of the room and through into the kitchen.

I turned to the window again and saw Dad's car, the one that had picked Mum up when we'd met in Hampton. It was parked, but I couldn't see anyone inside. I walked up to the window, pushing the curtains along so I could see better, but they must already have been at the door, as the next thing I heard was their knock.

I panicked. I put my glass down on the table, spilling the water. I wanted to get to the front door before Frances. I wanted to see Mum, to talk to her, find out what she wanted to give me. And as I moved, I saw it – the photograph – on the sideboard. Catherine. Her hair down, blowing around her face in the wind. She was smiling, laughing, standing on a rock, her arms out to the sides like she was balancing. I hadn't ever seen it before. There had never been any photographs here before. Frances must have set it out, for today. For Mum, for Dad, for me. And Catherine was smiling at me – my friend, my sister. I thought I might collapse under the weight of the feelings I had for her – and then I saw her face, again, in the water. Her hair splayed out all around her in the deep, black water, her eyes wide open with the shock. I felt a pain in the middle of my stomach like a punch, a repetitive punch. I couldn't breathe. I grabbed the arm of the chair next to me with both hands and I closed my eyes and started counting, counting, counting to try and bring myself back into the room.

Mum and Dad were in the hall now. I could hear them. They were about to come into the room. They were about to see me, like this.

I stood up.

The roof. I wanted to be on the roof. All I could think about, in that moment, was the roof, and being up high, and the space in my head, and the roof—

"Hello, Ana," Mum said and she smiled, but she looked so unsure of me as she said it, and it hurt.

"I got your message," I said.

"Good," she said.

I looked at Dad.

He nodded at me, his eyes to the floor. It was as much of a "Hello" as I was going to get, and he stood behind Mum, his tallness framing her perfectly.

"Please, sit down," said Frances. "Ana, come and help me with the tea things. And you'll need a cloth for that spillage."

I nodded, and followed her through to the kitchen.

"I can't believe they came," I said. "I mean – both of them. Dad too."

"They were both invited, Ana," Frances said.

"Yes, I know, but—"

"We are here so we can make things right," she said. "All of us. Now take this through. And don't cause a fuss." And she placed a tray of things in my hands. There was a pot of tea, a milk jug, sugar bowl, and the china – plates, cups and saucers.

As I walked into the room with the tray, Mum sat down. She neatly tucked her bag on the floor behind her feet and crossed her legs. She was upright, concentrating, looking at me all the time. Dad stood at the mantelpiece. His mug was still there. I remembered how the milk had turned, ready to fester. And I remembered my fall. And as I did my wound ached, and I looked down at the grate and saw my blood, dark and sticky around the edges, in the place where I'd hit my head. She'd left it there too. Like the mug. A spoil. I looked away.

And I caught a glimpse of the photograph again.

I'd killed her.

My friend.

The only sister I'd ever had.

And I'd killed her.

And we were back here, in this house, again.

And suddenly I wanted to stop this meeting from happening.

I wanted to make it all go away.

All that I knew and all that I'd done.

Because I regretted it.

I regretted it all.

"I need to go," I whispered urgently to Mum and Dad. "I don't think I can do this." As I said it I looked over my shoulder, to see if Frances was already on her way through from the kitchen. I knew what I had to do now. I had to get to the roof. I had to lie flat, feel the space and let myself go.

"What do you mean?" said Mum, her whole face taking on the wrinkled shape of her frown; a mass of lines and concern.

And then Frances came into the room with another tray – an old-fashioned sponge cake, spoons, forks and a knife laid out on it. She set it down awkwardly on the coffee table in front of us all.

We watched.

No one spoke.

Until Mum.

"It's been a long time," she said.

"Thirty-four years," Frances said.

There was more silence while Frances painstakingly poured the tea. The tension in the room was unbearable. I wanted to break the silence. I just wanted to scream, "I need to go! I need to leave!" but Frances's presence in the room was so strong I couldn't speak. I was too frightened even to move.

I could see that Dad was impatient, nervous. He was doing the thing he always did when he was waiting for something, shaking his leg slightly back and forth where he stood. It was like a rhythmic tick.

Everyone held their teacups and took a sip of tea. I couldn't bear the silence any longer.

"I need to go," I said. "This doesn't feel…right."

"I agree," said Dad.

"Why did you come, Richard?" Frances asked.

"For Amanda. Only for Amanda," Dad said, and I saw hurt – just for a moment – criss-cross Frances's face. "She wanted to come. But not on her own. I owed her," he said. "I owed her that."

"Owed her?" Frances said, and she scowled as she said it. "You stayed with her! You owe her nothing!"

"Yes, he did stay," Mum said. "In the end. But…it wasn't easy. And coming here today…" Her voice broke off.

I felt sick.

Sick panic rising up inside me.

I didn't want to be here, listening to them talk like this.

"So, Frances," said Mum, composing herself, "is there something specific you wanted to say to us all today – with Ana here? Is that why you invited us?"

"We are here to talk," Frances said. "We seem to be in a rather extraordinary situation and I thought it would be good for us to meet – together. It's been a long time. And Ana – she needs to know – she *wants* to know what happened—"

"I actually don't think I can do this," Dad said, putting down his cup and saucer.

"Me neither," I said. "I have to go."

"No, Ana!" said Frances.

I turned and faced my dad.

"I want to go," I said. "Please, let me go."

I wasn't sure why I felt I had to appeal to him, but I did.

He didn't look at me.

And I could see that he was caught. Mum and Frances both needed him to stay, and he was trapped, and he was hurting, just by being here, in the room.

"Why would you want to go now, Ana?" said Frances. "Why, when you have all of us here? Everyone who was here the night Catherine died? You do realize we're only here, now, thirty-four years later, because of you. We're here because you're asking for the truth, and now you have the gall to say that you don't want to hear it. I will not let you leave, Ana. Not until we've done what we came here to do."

I shook my head. She was wrong. I did want the truth, but I was frightened. I was so frightened. And the room was so quiet…

Frances turned towards me. "I would like you to tell us what happened to our child before she died, Ana. It's a perfectly reasonable request of someone who stands here and tells us she is Emma. Don't you agree, Richard?"

And then she turned to look at Dad before looking back again at me.

"You see, Catherine knew not to go near the river. She knew that. She always did what she was told, and I'd told her never to go near the river. So I want to know what happened. I want to know what made her go in."

"We're going to the river, Catherine. We'll play hide-and-seek by the river."

"If you don't play I'll tell on you. You have to come or that's what I'll do."

"Our daughter died too," said Mum, her words breaking through the ones in my head. "If Catherine hadn't been left in her care then maybe she would still be here today, Frances. Maybe they both would."

I looked up, at Mum.

"Well," said Dad as if he were hosting a chat show, "apparently she is! Apparently Emma's sitting right here with us today, just in someone else's body. How about that?"

Dad had moved from caught to angry.

He was never going to believe me. I knew that now.

"Stop being so facetious, Richard," said Mum, and her mouth went tight with hurt and rage. I couldn't tell if they still loved each other any more, but they had stayed together. Had they done that for me?

"If you can prove to me – if someone here, anyone, can prove to me – that this is Emma, then I'll have this conversation. I'll do it, Amanda," Dad said. "But I am not sitting here, dredging up the hell and guts of that night, on the basis that this girl, here, has bowled up and into our lives telling us she is *our* Emma!"

"Perhaps not everything in life adheres to your logic, Richard," said Frances. "I agree it would be easier if it did."

There was silence.

I wished I'd never come. I knew I should never have come. Not the first time, not the time after that, not now, not ever.

There was no place for me here.

"Ana?" said Frances. "Do you not have anything to say?"

I shook my head.

There was no place for me anywhere.

"You mean you have nothing to say? Nothing at all?"

"I told you. I don't know how I know the things I know," I said. "I can't show you or prove to you what I know. I can't explain the things that I know. I just know them." And as I spoke I thought only about the roof and the space and the run of the sky.

There.

On the roof.

There was a place for me there.

"I'm not sure I want to know what you know," said Mum. "What you know frightens me. Because if you're here, and you are Emma, then what? Can I take you home with me? Can I cook your favourite meal? Do all the things I've wanted to do for you and with you since you died… Do we become a family again? It's impossible… It's all beyond…anything…" she said, and she took a deep breath before she continued. "The thing is, I can't lose you again. I couldn't go through that again," she said, and she started to cry.

I wanted to go to her. Instinctively. I wanted to go to her.

"You're Emma and you're not Emma!" Mum said through her tears. "I'm not sure I can cope with that."

There was a moment of quiet. They looked at me – all of them. They were waiting to hear what I would say.

I looked back at them.

Mum was right. I was Emma and not Emma. I was Ana but not Ana. I was two people and yet, I was no one. And they – they were what? What were they to me, when I was no one?

Panic rose in my chest and closed my throat.

I couldn't breathe.

I wanted to leave.

I had to leave.

"I can't bring Catherine back," Frances said to me. "Can I? Even though I would do anything to have her back again with me."

There was a loud persistent thrumming in my head.

"If I were you, Amanda," said Frances, turning to face Mum. "I'd grab this girl with both my arms and I wouldn't let her go."

Let me go. Let me go. Let me go.

"Stop talking like this!" shouted Dad.

"Don't shout, Richard," Frances said.

"I will shout!" he said. "I will! Because I don't know what the hell we are all doing here! Just being here, in this house, it's..."

"...difficult?" said Frances, finishing his sentence. "I know. I live here. It's with me every day."

"It's just – it's just..." And he fumbled and ran his fingers through his hair. "For God's sake – Ana!" he said, spinning back around towards me. "Do you honestly believe what you are saying, yourself? Can you honestly say that you believe that you are Emma?"

I was nothing to him. I was no one. I knew that.

I didn't answer.

"I mean, we all know what happened, that night, with Catherine," he went on. "We were there." And he motioned to Mum and to Frances.

Not to me.

Because I was nothing. I was no one. And I knew that.

"What good does it do to go over it all again, to look to – I don't know – apportion blame now, for something that happened years ago…"

"BECAUSE *I* DON'T KNOW! MAYBE YOU ALL KNOW BUT I DON'T!" I screamed. "And I was there that night, and I'm here now, and – you don't have to believe me – but I'm walking around with this feeling, with this pain and this guilt. It overshadows everything. Can't you see that? CAN'T – YOU – SEE – THAT?" I screamed. "If you would just look at me, properly, you would see that!"

"Look at her, Richard, and look at me!" Frances said, quickly. "Because my grief, it still hangs over me like that. Exactly like that."

"Isn't that just how it is?" said Mum, looking at Frances. "We carry on living, but it's only ever half the life it was. Someone's cut the power supply, and you limp on, in dimmer light."

"I wasn't prepared to carry on living like that. Not then, and not now. I can't," I said.

Mum and Dad looked up at me, their eyes searching

my face. The atmosphere in the room had changed. I could feel it.

"No," Mum said. "Don't say that!"

"What do you mean?" said Dad. "What do you mean, when you say that?"

"You didn't do anything wrong," Mum said. "I always told her that, didn't I, Richard?" She appealed to Dad now, just as I had done before. "I told you that. I know I did!"

Dad nodded.

"But it was wrong that Catherine died, Amanda," said Frances. "It was wrong! And now Ana is here, and there must be a reason why she is here. Catherine would never have gone near the river. Never. Emma killed her. And that's why Emma's here – why she's come back."

"We're going to the river, Catherine. We'll play hide-and-seek by the river."

"If you don't play I'll tell on you. You have to come or that's what I'll do."

"The inquest dealt with it, at the time, Frances," said Dad. "You know that. It was an accidental death. You have to accept it. Don't make this any harder than it already is. Please, Frances, don't do that." And his face creased with the pain as he pleaded, but still, he wouldn't look at me.

Mum was looking at me, all the time.

"You were only twenty-two when you died," she said. "You had so much more life to live."

"But I killed her!" I said. "I killed Catherine! I don't know how I could have done something so wrong, but I did. I killed her!"

"No! Ana! No! You didn't!" Mum said.

I drew in a breath, I sobbed, and my whole body heaved with the force of it.

"Ana, you didn't kill her! You didn't kill Catherine!" she said again. "You didn't kill her! I told you that back then, and I'm telling you again now. You didn't kill her!" And Mum grabbed both of my hands and I thought I would be sick with the loss and the love and the longing for the truth.

"Why do you think that you killed her?" Mum said.

"Because of how I feel – because of the things I remember," I said.

"You see, Amanda, she knows she did it. She just doesn't remember," said Frances. "That's why we are here. So we can tell her!"

"So tell me!" I said, and I stood up, letting go of Mum's hands as I did.

I wanted to scream and yell and howl and fill the room with my noise until someone told me what I'd done.

"Just tell me!" I screamed. "For God's sake, just someone tell me!" The screaming was burning my throat now, fear and confusion were dancing hot rough flames across my throat. I started to cry, to sob. "What happened? What did I do to her? Just tell me!"

Dad looked up – at me – and then at Mum.

There was quiet before Mum spoke again.

"You didn't kill Catherine," Mum said.

"You didn't kill her," Dad said. "The only person you killed was yourself."

And then he broke down, his body falling against Mum's where she sat, and it was the fall of a giant but gently felled tree –

and I felt the brutality of his fall

– all of it –

just as I had felt my own

when I had taken my life

for Catherine's

when I had been Emma

– and still –

I was falling now

in the new knowledge of what I had done.

41.

"Well!" said Frances, and she smiled a slow smile. "The girl who says she is Emma – she didn't know!"

"Frances!" Mum said, her hand resting on Dad's back. "Don't be so cruel."

"Catherine's was an accidental death," said Dad, again. He sounded numb, exhausted.

"But there was no one there but me. It had to be me," I said. "It had to be me. Didn't it? Frances – you said it was me? You told me, that night, that it was me – it was because of me—"

"You what?" said Mum, looking now at Frances.

"I told her," Frances repeated. "She's right. I told her."

"She was nine years old!" screamed Mum, and her voice cracked with emotion as she said it.

"Yes," said Frances.

"Why did you do that, Fran?" asked Dad, his face a mess of confusion.

"Don't you remember?" I said, looking at Mum.

"What?"

"Frances talking to me, in the porch?"

"When?"

"You were in the street with Dad, arguing with Dad," I said. "I was waiting for you at the house. There were people everywhere, and the police were stood by the gate. I couldn't get to you..."

"When?" Mum said.

"After. After Catherine was found," I said, and I started to cry, and I was crying now, for me. Not for Catherine, but for me.

"You never told me that," Mum said, her voice was so soft and quiet now. "I never knew."

"What did Frances say?" asked Dad.

"That it was me, that Catherine was dead, that it was because of me. She said she'd seen me. It was my fault. And she was right. I mean, I wanted you, Dad. I wanted you all to myself. I didn't want to play with Catherine. I took Catherine to the river and she didn't want to go and I told her to hide so that I could come back to the house on my own, to find you, to play with you on my own. Except when I came back you didn't answer and I saw you together, you and Frances, and—"

"You saw them? Dad and Frances? Together?" Mum said, her voice rising now.

"Yes. I peeked through the letter box. I'd come to get Dad.

No one answered the door, so I looked through the letter box and I saw them," I said, crying. "I didn't mean to see them. I just wanted Dad to come and play. After that, I didn't know what to do – I'd left Catherine at the river, in the dark. I'd left her. So I hid. I hid behind the bins, until you found me, because I didn't know what else to do."

"I never knew…" said Mum. She was shaking. "I never knew any of this. If I'd known what you'd seen – what Frances had said to you – it changes everything – it could have changed everything, if I'd known…" Her voice was slow, hopeless.

"Rubbish!" said Frances. "They were playing together –" she motioned carelessly with her hand towards me – "your Emma and my Catherine. They went out to play together, and Emma was looking after Catherine, and Catherine came back dead."

"It – was – an – accident!" screamed Mum, through her own tears now.

"Of course you would say that. I understand why you want to protect her. She's your daughter. But tell me, who protected mine?" said Frances.

"You left them!" shouted Mum. "You and Richard left Catherine and Emma outside, on their own, so you could be together! It was wrong what you did!"

"You can't go on protecting Emma now, Amanda," said Frances. "Not now when she stands here in front of us racked with her guilt. You say it was an accident – but how can you know that? How can any of us know that?"

"I have to believe it was an accident," said Dad. "I have to."

"But we don't know," said Frances. "We weren't there. Only Emma can really know what happened. She was the last one to see Catherine alive. And, look at her! She feels so guilty. So guilty that she came back. She came to me, she found me. She asked me for help. And I gave it – I am giving it now – just as she asked – so that you can know what I have always known – that she killed her."

"That's your version of the truth, Frances!" said Mum. "It's what you want to believe. It's not what happened."

"Someone has to be responsible!" shouted Frances.

"We were *all* responsible!" screamed Mum.

"Don't say that," said Dad. "Don't say it!" And he bowed his head down again. He was broken.

"Richard," said Mum, trying to pull him up.

"I know," he said. "I know what I did. And I lost – so much. I lost it all. I lost them both – Emma and Catherine."

"Well, I am not responsible!" said Frances.

"Yes, you are!" screamed Mum. "You are! You were here, you and Richard. Both of you were here, the whole time, but you weren't watching the girls. You can't pretend that that didn't happen, that it didn't matter, Frances. It mattered!"

I turned, and leaned in towards Mum, so our faces were close and I could see right into the colour of her eyes. "So no one killed Catherine? Is that what you're saying? It was an accident? No one killed her?"

Dad leaned across Mum and he reached over to me and took both my hands. They were warm, and his touch, it was still familiar. "It was an accident," he said. "A terrible accident."

"But I told her to go and hide," I said, and I cried again as I said it. "Because I wanted you all to myself. I didn't want to share you with anyone. I went back to the house to find you. I left Catherine by the river, hiding—"

"That doesn't mean you killed her, Ana," said Mum.

"I wish I hadn't—"

"What?" said Dad.

"You pushed her – didn't you – you pushed her and she fell and you held her down so she stayed under the water," said Frances. "You held her under until she coughed and cried. You held her under until she died!"

"No – I don't remember that," I cried. "I don't remember doing that!"

"I'm right," said Frances, "I know I'm right! You were always the jealous one. You said it yourself. You wanted your dad all to yourself. You didn't want him to be with me. So you punished Catherine!"

"But you weren't *with* Catherine when she died!" said

Mum, looking at me now. "Emma wasn't with her when she died! You didn't kill her. It doesn't matter what you said or how you felt about Dad. You didn't kill her!"

"You are here for a reason—" Frances said.

"But I don't remember—" I said.

"You were with *me*," said Mum.

"You pulled me up from behind the wall – you hurt me – you were cross," I said to Mum.

"I was," Mum said, "but not with you. With Dad, with Frances. I'd gone to look for you and I'd come to the house and there was no answer and I found you, behind the bins. I took you back with me, to the party. I wanted you with me."

"But I left Catherine," I said. "We were playing hide-and-seek. I left her—"

"That's the game," said Mum. "To go and hide!"

"And you were so cross with me – and I couldn't tell you what I had seen, when I'd looked through the letter box. I was scared – I didn't like it – and I'd left Catherine—"

"I was cross with Dad!" Mum said. "Not with you. I was cross with him for leaving you on your own. I knew where he was, and what he was doing. As soon as I saw you outside, on your own, I knew he had to be with Frances. I wasn't blind. I'd seen the way they'd looked at each other for years. But I didn't want you with me when I spoke to Dad. The things I had to say to him – they were not for you to hear. I didn't think about where Catherine was then. I don't know why. I was angry, not thinking straight. Maybe that was it. And I regret that… I took you back to the party and went to speak to Dad. I wasn't cross with you, darling. I was cross with Dad!"

"I didn't know that—"

"No – you wouldn't have done. You were a child. Remember – a child!"

"And you left *my* child out there, in the darkness," said Frances.

"No, Frances!" said Mum. "You did that. You and Richard. Not Emma."

"When did she die?" I said.

"The coroner estimated time of death around seven thirty," said Dad.

"You were with me at that time," said Mum. "I took you from behind the bins and we went back to the party. You were with me."

"No!" said Frances. "That's not what happened!"

"You were with me, Ana," said Mum, putting her hands around my face, and pulling it towards her so I was looking right into the blue of her eyes. "You weren't anywhere near Catherine when she died. You didn't kill her. Why would you? You were a good, kind girl."

I looked at Dad. His face was crumpled, like someone had trodden all over it.

"But I saw her," I said. "In the water—"

"You should never have seen what you saw," said Dad.

"But I did," I said. "And I see her face now – all the time."

"That's my fault," said Mum. "I should never have taken you with me to look for her. But when I asked you, you said you could show me where you and Catherine had been playing, and it was so dark I thought if you could show me, we'd find her, quicker."

Mum paused and looked at Frances.

"I knew when I left Emma at the party and I came back to your house that you were with my husband, Frances. I had probably known for some time, but I wasn't prepared to accept it until that night. When I came back to the house I saw you both, together. You kissed as you stood on the front step. I told you I had Emma, and then I asked you where Catherine was – if I hadn't, would you have even thought to look for her? Don't you dare suggest that I left your child out there in the darkness, Frances! Don't you dare! I went out and I took Emma and we looked for your daughter. *We* looked for her! And *we* found her. Me and Emma. And I wish that we'd never found her like we did. For me, and for Emma. Because then, maybe, Emma would have had a better chance at living. Maybe she'd still be alive, now. My darling Emma."

I looked up again, at Mum.

"I didn't kill her. I didn't kill Catherine..." I said.

Mum shook her head.

"I killed myself..." I said.

Mum's face creased up as she closed her eyes in acknowledgement. There was no relief here. I might not have killed Catherine, but to see the look on Mum's face now was almost more than I could bear.

"We tried so hard to understand how you felt – depression – your battle with it – it was always there," Mum said. "Seeing Catherine's body like you did in the water, it ruined you. You were plagued by it. You felt responsible. And nothing I could do or say could change that."

"We failed," said Dad. "We let you down." He didn't look up. He was weeping into his hands. Filling them with tears.

I hadn't killed Catherine.

I'd killed myself.

The horror of it seeped in.

"I'm sorry," I said. "I'm so, so sorry..."

"You don't need to be sorry," Mum said.

"But I took my life. I must have –" and I paused – "hurt you...so much..." And as I said it I thought about Rachel, and how she would feel if I'd done this to her, and I couldn't bear to even think of it, of the pain.

"There is nothing for you to be sorry for," Mum said. "We loved you so much. We felt so desperate that we couldn't help you, that we just never got the chance—" And she broke off.

"And I," Frances said, "I have heard your apology and it means nothing!" She almost spat as she said it.

And then she screamed.

It was rasping and loud and desperate.

"I will never forgive you!" she said. "You crucified us all, Emma. All of us. And now you are here – you are actually here – to face it! Amanda and Richard might say that there is nothing for you to be sorry for, but how can they say that? Really? How can they mean it? You broke their hearts. And you broke mine too when you killed Catherine!"

She stood and she picked up the knife from the tray in front of her, and in one quick movement she bent down to where I was sitting and she held the knife to my neck.

I felt the cold point, the sharpness, the pressure as the tip threatened to gently pierce my skin like a needle in a balloon…and I wasn't sure what was happening and I looked at Dad, for an answer, because I didn't understand.

"Frances!" Mum screamed, and she stood up.

"Frances, for God's sake! What are you doing? Put the knife down!" Dad said. I could hear panic in his voice.

"I won't put it down. I will not!" said Frances.

"It's not her fault," screamed Mum. "It was never her fault!"

"No one has ever given me an explanation!" screamed Frances. "And then Emma came to me! And she must die for what she did. It is the only way to make this right!"

Dad took a step towards Frances. But Frances's hand was still on the knife, and I began to feel pain from the pressure. It was running through my nerves now, cold and sharp, and it was careering through my body and dancing on my brain. I thought my head might split open with it – the clear point and the fine edges of the knife pressing my skin—

"I've lost two daughters!" Dad screamed. "Two! And I can tell you now – this will never make things right! Never! Put it down, Frances! Put the knife down!"

"It has to be over now!" Mum screamed. "It has to be!" And she held out her hand – for the knife – and when Frances didn't respond – she leaned forward and she took it. In one strong and quick movement she removed the knife from Frances's hand, from my neck. And I could see that it had taken all the strength she had left inside her to do it.

She had saved me.

My mum.

She had saved me.

42.

I twitched as the knife left my skin, and I thought I might collapse. But I didn't. I lifted my palms up to my neck, to feel it.

It was smooth. Uncut. Still, I didn't want to take my hand away from my neck. I might not have been cut, but I couldn't get rid of the feeling of sharp metal on my skin. I wanted to rub the feeling off me somehow.

Frances turned to face me.

I could feel my pulse in my hand, in my neck. I could hear the beat of it loud in my ears. I counted the seconds to the beat. One, two, three, four… One, two, three, four… One, two, three, four…

"Ana!" I could hear Mum's voice, calling me. "Ana – come – with me… Come on," she whispered.

"Don't let them go, Richard!" said Frances. "Stop them! I haven't finished yet!"

"No," said Dad. "No! This is enough!"

"You can't leave!" Frances screamed. "None of you can leave!"

"Ana!" Mum had taken my hand and she was helping me to stand.

"You don't understand!" said Frances. "Why don't any of you understand? I – have – nothing!" she screamed, and as she did her voice cracked like stone breaking bone.

It hurt me, all of me, to hear it.

I looked at her, where I stood. Her dry eyes, her sallow skin, her entire face – twisted. I'd seen that look before, many times, but I'd never recognized it until then. It was hate – and it was unmistakable, now that I knew.

"It – will – never – be – over," she said, looking Amanda directly in the face. "Whatever you said, whatever you just did, to save her, it will never be over."

"You're wrong, Frances," said Mum, holding me up. "It's over now. It's completely over." And she turned her back on Frances and looked at me.

"Ana, if you are the person you say you are – if you are Emma, and you came back – then I'm glad. I'm glad that I can take you by the hand and tell you that I loved you, and tell you that I am sorry. Because had I known what Frances had said that night, if I'd known that she'd told you it was your fault, I would have fought her with my own bare hands until she took the words back. I would have fought her to the death. I would have done that for you – I would have done anything – and at least now you can know that. I can say it, and you can know it."

I thought about Rachel, and I knew, if this was me and Rachel, Rachel would have done that too. She would have done that for me too.

"So I'm glad," Mum said. "I'm glad that I met you – Ana – Emma – whoever you are. I'm truly glad."

I felt so light-headed. My legs were shaking, weak. I didn't want to pass out but I could feel myself sinking, lower and lower. I just wanted to get to the floor. To feel the solidness of the floor beneath me. To let it hold me.

I knew I was going to collapse. I could feel myself begin to go.

I looked at Dad.

"Amanda!" he said to Mum. "Hold on to Ana! Hold her!"

Mum was trying to hold me up but I was too heavy in her arms. I could feel that I was. She was struggling to hold me.

"Can you take her?" Dad said to Mum. "If you can, I'll deal with Frances."

Mum nodded.

"Find out where she lives – get her home," he said and he looked up at me, and I blinked at him. A slow blink. In agreement, in regret, because a slow blink was all I could manage. And I realized, as I began to make my way across the room, towards the door, that when Mum closed the sitting-room door behind us, I was unlikely to ever see him again. And I didn't have the strength or the courage in that moment to tell him that I loved him.

Mum sat me down on a chair in the hall. I couldn't take another step. Not just yet. I needed a few moments of rest before I stood again.

"I'm sorry," I said to Mum. "I'm so sorry." And I started to cry.

"No!" said Mum. "Don't be sorry. You don't need to be sorry. You need to be strong now."

"I should never have taken my life – I should never have done that to myself – to you – and to Dad..." And as I said it I leaned forwards and rested my forehead on her shoulder. I was so tired.

"Let me look at you," Mum said and she turned me to the side, and she looked at my neck. "You're okay," she said. "You're okay."

"You must hate me," I said, still crying.

She shook her head. "No!"

"I hate me," I said. "For what I did."

"Don't say that! You were the most wonderful girl."

"But these feelings, these feelings that I've done the most terrible thing – if I didn't kill Catherine, then—"

"You took your life, Ana. You didn't kill Catherine, but your life – it was not your own after we found her body in the water. And you took the decision that it was not worth living. You tried. You tried so hard to live, to be happy and to live. But ultimately, you couldn't. Not with what you knew – or at least with what you thought you knew – and with what you'd seen." She paused. "I so wanted to help you, but I couldn't…" And she broke down and cried.

I took her hand.

"Frances has so much to answer for," Mum said, through her tears. "If only I'd known what she'd said to you…" And she bit her lip, hard.

I squeezed her hand. I was surprised at my strength.

"I want you to have this," she said, and she pulled out a letter from her jacket pocket and pressed it into the palm of my hand.

"What is it?"

"It's the thing I wanted you to have. The thing I mentioned on the phone. I kept it. I don't know why. Maybe it was always meant for you. I don't know. Anyway, you should have it. I want you to have it."

"But why?"

"Because she never did. It never got to her. Not in time. I was too late."

I nodded.

"You should go," she said. "Go home." And as she went to the front door to open it for me, Dad came into the hall.

We both turned and stood, in silence, and looked at him.

"She's still angry. She's raging. You should go, Ana."

"Dad?" I said, my voice a whisper.

He looked at me.

"I love you."

"So go now," he said. "Just go. Be safe. There is no reason for you to come back here again. You know the truth now." And he took my hand and he squeezed it tight – and in that squeeze I felt the strength of his love. I knew it was all he could give me, but it was everything to me that he'd done it – it was more than enough. I squeezed his hand back as tightly as I could, and then he turned and left to go back to Frances in the sitting room.

"He's right," Mum said. "You must go."

"But, Mum?" I said, and I sobbed. "I want you, Mum – I don't want to leave you – I can't lose you – I've missed you – so much…"

"And you found me," she said. "You found me. And now, you must go."

"But I don't want to—"

"You must," she said. "For me. You must go now, for me."

And she smiled at me. A tired smile, and I remembered her smile, and how much I liked it, and how good it made me feel.

"Ana?" she said.

"Yes?"

"This is goodbye, darling."

I looked at her.

"Goodbye," she said.

"Goodbye," I said.

And I turned.

And I left.

And at last…

we had said goodbye.

43.

I walked out onto the Green, and sat behind the oak and I reached into my bag for my phone and dialled home.

"Hello?" Rachel answered immediately.

"Rachel – it's me." I was crying.

"Ana! Where are you? Where have you been? They said you weren't at school – I've been calling you—"

"Can you come and get me?" I said.

"Yes! Yes – are you okay?"

I couldn't speak, for the tears.

"Ana! Just tell me, are you okay?"

"Yes," I sobbed. "I'm okay."

"Where are you?"

"Teddington. The Avenue, in Teddington," I said.

I took a deep breath in.

"Don't be cross, Rachel. Please don't be cross."

"I'm coming. Now!" she said.

"Thank you, Rachel. Thank you."

"I'm on my way," she said. "I'm already on my way."

I hung up.

I looked down at the letter in my hand. It was addressed to Emma. It was still sealed. She had never opened it. I opened it, while I waited. And I read.

17 October 1994

My Darling Emma,

I got your letter this morning, and am just so sad. I had no idea that you were feeling the things you are feeling – still, now, all these years later. I've been trying to think of what I can do to make it better. But I've realized that this is something I just can't mend or fix or soothe. Not for you, not for me, not for anyone. What happened to Catherine that night was too awful, too painful. I can't go on pretending that it wasn't. Perhaps I haven't been there for you enough. Perhaps I haven't listened enough. Perhaps it will help if I tell you that even I sometimes find it hard to accept that Catherine is gone. Unless we go back, and somehow miraculously change the past, or rewrite history, we have to accept that she is gone. This is a lesson in life, and I'm learning it with you. I know I tell you not to wish, that wishes don't come true, that they are flippant things, but if I could have one wish it would be for you – not for me. And it would be to make what happened that day with Catherine less painful for you. If I could change anything – if I could go back and change one thing – I would never have taken you with me to look for her at the river. It's my fault that you saw what you saw that night. I know it wouldn't change what happened, but you should never have seen her in the river. And I am so, so sorry for that. But I had no idea what had happened. I didn't know that we would find her, as we did. Just like you didn't know, when you went out to play on the Green, that a game of hide-and-seek would end like it did. What happened cannot ever in any way be your fault, Emma. You have to remember that. You have to believe it. It never was, it never could have been. I have to tell myself the same thing, when I think of you feeling so very bad and I remember that in part, I am to blame.

I am leaving work early tomorrow and I will be with you by 3 p.m. Just think, by the time you are reading this I'll almost be with you. I'll take you out – fish and chips, curry, pizza whatever you want! We'll talk. I'll bring those photos you love of me and Grandad on the beach in 1961 – the ones where we all look miserable and it's cold and you can't believe what I'm wearing. They always make you laugh! I'll do anything I can to make it better for you, Emma. Anything at all. I can't wait to see you. I love you, darling. Don't ever forget that.

Mum xxxx

I held the letter in my hands. The paper was soft. I didn't want to let it go. I lay down on my back to look up at the sky. It felt so good to lie down. To feel the earth beneath me. I let myself stare into the blue. The sky was clear and crisp. It was beautiful. Beautiful like Emma was beautiful. Beautiful Emma. Good, kind, Emma.

I let myself blink.

I had a chance. I had a chance to be beautiful too. And now, I would take it. I would grasp it with both hands and I would never let it go. Because I wanted to live now. I knew, in that moment, that I wanted to live. I wanted to live until I was old. I wanted to live until my skin wrinkled and my eyes went cloudy and my hands curled up like claws. I just wanted to live. And I wanted to see what Spain looked like, and work out why my name had only one "n" in it, and I wanted to get more Converse before I went... and died again... I wanted to live boisterously, wildly, loudly... I wanted to make new memories and lock the old ones up in a place that they would never be found, a place where no one would discover them. A place that Rachel knew nothing about...because she didn't have to know. She didn't have to know about any of it... All I had to do was stay here...stay conscious... And let her find me...

Please, I wished, *let Rachel find me...let her find me... let my mother find me...*

44.

Rachel found me.

When she did I reached out to her and held on to her like I'd never held on to her before.

"What happened?" she said, crying. "What happened to you?" And I didn't reply. I just let her hold me and hug me and stroke my hair, and she didn't let me go and I liked it because I didn't want her to let me go. Not now. Not ever.

She helped me up onto my feet and we started to walk. I felt so weak. It took all the energy I had to put one foot in front of the other and make it over to the car.

"We'll go home," Rachel said. "We'll get you home, and then we'll talk," she said, and she leaned over and stroked my face before she started the car, and I let her.

As we moved away from The Avenue I looked over to the houses in the street.

This place had been part of my life – before – my first life.

It didn't need to be part of my life now.

I laid my head down against the seat belt and I closed my eyes and I slept.

I wasn't far from home, but still, I slept all the way.

45.

Jamie forgave me for being weird, for walking away. He came to the house that night with a present.

"What's this for?" I said, smiling.

"Your birthday," he said.

"That's not for months!"

"I know. I just couldn't wait," he said and he put a box on my lap and opened up the lid to reveal a new pair of Converse. Silver sequins. Size four. They were perfect.

"Wow!" I said. "These must have cost you the earth!"

"Yeah, well...most of my savings," he said, looking at the floor.

"Thank you," I said, and I took his hand, and with my other hand I lifted his face to mine. "Really. Thank you."

He came closer to me. "Please," he said, "just don't run off like that again. It frightened me, to see you like that."

I nodded. "I know," I said. "Me too."

And we kissed.

And in that kiss I felt like anything and everything were possible. I wasn't scared any more. And that feeling, that I was somehow darkened by just being alive, it had gone. I was in the present now. There was an immense rush in just being, in each and every moment. If I could have held myself close to Jamie, moulded myself into him, I would have done it. But I didn't. Not yet. Instead I spoke.

"I'm glad you came," I said. "I'm glad that you can forgive me."

"I'm glad too," he said, and he smiled and I smiled and we smiled so much we couldn't kiss any longer.

Frances had a stroke. Grillie told me she'd died almost instantly, at home. A massive bleed to the brain that no one could have prevented, that no one could have foreseen. Grillie told me she was shocked, but that she'd decided that we shouldn't be too sad. "She went quickly. She'd lived a long life," she said. I nodded. I couldn't argue with that. I just hoped that if there was any such thing as justice, Frances would see Catherine again. Perhaps in some other world, some other life. And I hoped that for me, she and I were done, and that we would never ever have to meet again.

* * *

I promised Rachel there would be no more disappearing acts, no bunking off school, that nothing like that would happen again. It took me a couple of weeks to prove it, but I did.

I was kinder to her too. I liked her – I mean, I'd always liked her – but without the comparison to Mum and Dad, there was more room for her, if that makes sense. And she was a cool mum. We did stuff together, we hung out at home, and even when she annoyed me, she never annoyed me like she had done before. Did I love her more? No, I don't think I did. But I loved her better, if that's possible. I didn't resent or begrudge her love for me any more. I would never take her love for granted again.

Rachel never knew what happened that day, at Frances's, and I figured she would never need to. I think we both felt that something had changed, after that day. That there was some tangible difference in the way we were now. We never talked about it. But Grillie did. She'd come around every second Friday and have dinner with Rachel, Jamie and me and she'd say, "I don't know whether it's Jamie or your mother or you, but you seem happier, Ana, and I like it! Keep doing what you're doing, girl!" And she'd wink at me.

And I'd look at Jamie, and he'd grin, and Rachel would nod and say, "I know what you mean, Grillie. Long may it last!" And I'd just let them all keep thinking whatever they were thinking, believe whatever they were believing, and be glad that I was alive and that I was me.

"Don't forget that you're young – blessedly young; be glad of it on the contrary and live up to it. Live all you can; it's a mistake not to. It doesn't so much matter what you do in particular, so long as you have your life. If you haven't had that what have you had?"

Henry James, *The Ambassadors*

acknowledgements

I'd like to say a huge and heartfelt thank you to the following people:

To Robert Bird for giving me the time and the support that allowed me to write this book; without you it would never have happened. To my mum, Lyn Dougherty, for giving me my love of reading from such an early age, and for her unfailing encouragement as soon as I started to write. To The Faberites for being the best writing group a girl could ever have; we got so lucky the day we signed up for that Faber Academy course. And in particular to Michelle Wood, Emma Higham and Caroline Gerard, who read not just chunks but whole drafts along the way. To Anthony McGowan for teaching that course – a crucial part of all our luck – and for making me brave enough to give the writing a go. To Hilary Delamere at The Agency, whose passion and belief in the book, right from the start, has been quite frankly amazing. I am so glad that we're doing this together. I honestly couldn't have wished for it to be any other way. And finally to the team at Usborne Publishing for taking *My Second Life* on board and guiding it so beautifully through to publication. Particular thanks must go to Anne Finnis, whose considered and insightful notes enabled this book to become so much better than I ever hoped it might be.

a note from the author

The inspiration for this book came from a brief conversation with my son when he was nine. He was talking to me while he lay in the bath about something that had gone wrong for him that day at school, and he said "I wish you could rewind life". And there was something in that wish and the answer that I gave him – "Yes, I know, that would be great, wouldn't it? But you just can't do that" – which struck me as the beginning of something.

So I sort of let my thoughts stew for a while and an idea came to me. What if you were a fifteen-year-old girl and you knew that you'd lived before? But not only that, you knew that you'd done something terrible in your first life, and you had to find out what you had done to make sense of your second life, your life *now*.

The idea that you could live more than once has always fascinated me, and I think you can come across people in life who simply appear to have been born wise. They just seem to have a knowledge, an understanding, an acceptance of life that makes them this way. And sometimes you can meet a child who has this kind of wisdom, and it seems to me a mystery as to where it has come from – because they haven't lived enough life yet for it to have come from experience. And I like to wonder: can a child, a person, come into this world with the layers of another life embedded deep within them? Is somehow the fabric of who they are in this life woven with the essence of who they were in a life before?

So the idea of having lived before isn't about simply saying "I was an Arabian prince" or "I was a Victorian pauper"; it's not just about what you did or who you were – rich, poor, good, bad. It's about the experiences and emotions, maybe even the integrity, that having lived before might bring to living a second life in the here and now. And that's what I wanted to explore in writing this book.

about the author

Faye Bird worked as a literary agent representing TV and film screenwriters before becoming a writer herself. She lives in London with her husband and their two children. *My Second Life* is her first novel.

If you loved My Second Life, you might also like...

"Riveting."
The Independent on Sunday

Celia Frost is a freak. At least that's what everyone thinks. Her life is ruled by a rare disorder that means she could bleed to death from the slightest cut, confining her to a gloomy bubble of "safety". No friends. No fun. No life.

But when a knife attack on Celia has unexpected consequences, her mum reacts strangely – and suddenly they're on the run. Why is her mum so scared? Someone out there knows. And when they find Celia, she's going to wish the truth was a lie.

A buried secret, a gripping manhunt, a dangerous deceit... What is the truth about Celia Frost?

ISBN 9781409531098

A mesmerizing psychological thriller with the most incredible twist you'll read all year.

Three years ago, thirteen-year-old Danny Geller vanished without trace.

His family and friends are still hanging on to every last shred of hope. Not knowing if he's alive or dead, their world is shrouded in shadows, secrets and suspicions.

This is the story of what happens when hope comes back to haunt you. When your desperation is used against you. When you search for the truth – but are too scared to accept the reality staring you in the face.

Because sometimes perhaps it's better to live in the dark.

ISBN 9781409563693

powerful...
captivating...
brave...